ORPHANS AFIELD

A NOVEL OF THE CIVIL WAR ON THE TEXAS
FRONTIER

J. ARTHUR EIDSON

Note to the Reader:

This book is fiction. Though it is based on historic events, and it attempts to accurately reflect the times and people, it is not an exact record. However, the most outlandish depictions contained herein, are in fact those most closely related to the historic event. Texas was deeply divided during the Civil War. Many counties, especially in northeast Texas were anti-secession. Anti-unionist vigilantes declared guerrilla war against the "Lincolnites". This gave rise to a civil war within the Civil War. Great strife and sorrow ensued.

This book is dedicated to all the costly choices we made. May we never repeat them.

CHAPTER 1

Esker Doyle was tired of contending with the sticky black soil. Though it was fall in East Texas, it was hot enough to break a sweat. The weather was muggy, and flies so dense on the white mule, its rump looked gray. Recent rains had churned out late flies and turned the black clay into glue. The plow would not scour, and he spent more time scraping it than he did plowing. He only made twenty or thirty feet before the plowshare caked in mud and lost its bite. It was getting dark, anyway, and he unhitched the mule and led her to her stall. He stood by the mule shed and watched the Sulphur River bottoms get dark. A barred owl called. A little strip of yellow sky still held out above the forest, but had blinked out to dark before he got to the cabin, a dog run with a kitchen tacked on the back. His father waited for him on the porch.

"How far today, Esker?" Pap asked, and exhaled blue smoke from his pipe.

He was thin and bearded, and since being stepped on by an ox, had not done much more than smoke and watch his boys work from the porch.

"Not more than an acre. The field is still too wet, Pap. The plow won't scour."

Esker scraped mud from his shoes and muttered into his shirt front. Pap grunted, stood and turned to the cabin door.

"I expect we shall do better in the morning, Esker," he said over his shoulder as he went in for his supper.

1

Esker resented that there was little *we* about it. He would take turns with his brothers, while Pap shouted instructions or criticism from the porch. He danced around and waved his arms so, that Esker was certain he was energetic enough to plow. He still liked to sow corn, though, and planted it with a stick, a few seeds at a time. This field would go to wheat, so getting the seedbed prepared was urgent; the sowing needed no later than the end of October.

Since they had not yet slaughtered the hog, supper was what had been canned the previous summer, and beans and cornbread. His younger brothers were fat, though strong. The youngest they called Pie for his fondness for it, and the other Poochy, though Esker was not sure why. They both plowed better than him, though he was three years older than the next. Their appetites were remarkable, and one did not get between either of them and their food, which noisily and quickly disappeared from the table. Esker was thin and phlegmatic like his father, while his brothers were stout and energetic like their mother. He was bookish, too, though he had long ago exhausted the supply standing on the fireplace mantle, being more for decoration than use. There was a Bible, a copy of Pilgrim's Progress, McGuffey's 3rd and 4th Readers, a New England Primer and a few others. His father kept one book close and never mentioned it, let alone displayed it. It was the autobiography of Frederick Douglass.

The weather improved, the field was prepared and wheat sown by the prescribed date. By the time the little green shoots emerged from the black soil, the evenings were cool and nights cold and most of the farm work over. Pap entertained the older male portion of the neighborhood on his porch. Even in the evening gloom under the eave, Esker knew they were there by the pall of blue smoke and the glow from their pipes and cigars. Three or four old men gathered at a time to smoke and spit tobacco juice, drink from a jug and talk politics. Abraham Lincoln was the main topic, his election being the most momentous news in the past several years. Most in the neighborhood attended the Methodist Church, which was occasionally led by a circuit-riding pastor from Kansas, and most of his congregation was more or less recently immigrated from the Midwest and held on to their views on slavery and the sanctity of the Union. Though the talk was often loud, the opinions were considered subversive by a good portion of Texas.

Esker and his brothers took advantage of the end of the field season and repaired to the woods along the river to hunt. The household possessed a single shotgun, and the boys took turns with it, bringing home mainly squirrels, but occasionally a possum for the pot. Roast possum and potatoes was Maw's favorite, and she baked it up brown and tender. Since their reach of the Sulphur River had settled, varmints such as possums were scarce. Deer had fled the area entirely, and buffalo had not been seen in a generation.

Esker enjoyed the trip to the river bottoms more than the hunting itself. Late in fall, beyond the field edge, the red and yellow prairie grasses stood head high to Esker, the more so for Poochy and Pie, who stood on their toes to get their bearings. The boys descended the three river terraces. The woods got thicker on each one. In the bottoms the trees reached out across the river, forming a gallery where their limbs met and intertwined. Water oaks, pecans and red oaks made enough feed to keep all three of the family's hogs in good shape and fat by the time December slaughter came.

Pie shot three squirrels and they were cleaning them when the men rode up. All three riders grinned at the boys, but the grins were more a baring of tobacco-stained teeth than smiles.

The first rider asked, "You shoot them squirrels, did ye?"

He, along with his friends, each had a red feather stuck in his hatband. The speaker was young, bearded and fat, and his feather bobbed when he talked. He carried a big brass pistol in his belt.

Pie replied, without looking up from his sack, that he had indeed shot them, and they were on the way home to get them fried up. Pie put the last squirrel in the sack and held it tight. Esker did not know the men, but he had seen them in the neighborhood. The other riders flanked their spokesman, and encircled the boys.

"You're the boys of that crazy man, ain't ye?" asked the man with the gun in his belt. "You're the boys of that crazy man what will lay down for that ugly cur of a Lincoln."

He spat tobacco juice at the boys, but misjudged the wind. He wiped his shirtfront and face with a rag. It did not improve his mood. He pulled the pistol from his belt and pointed it at the boys.

"You get outta here, and tell your son-of-a-bitch of a paw that we are watchin' him." The horsemen rode through their midst and ascended the river terrace. The brothers exhaled and looked at each other.

Pie pointed at his younger brother's crotch. "Poochy pissed his pants!"

"Did not," hissed Poochy. "Just a little squirrel blood."

The argument continued up the slope and home and until they presented the squirrels to Maw, who grinned at the boys and began to grease a skillet. Esker knew he was her favorite without being told. Her eyes twinkled when she looked at him. She often saved scrapings from pans or other tasty bits for him.

It was Esker's job to tell his father about the confrontation on the river, he being the oldest.

"What did they look like?" asked Pap, who otherwise nodded and did not look sufficiently alarmed to Esker. He described the men. The only information which seemed to get his father's attention was their wearing of the red feathers.

Esker was sufficiently alarmed for both, and asked, "Don't you think we might get us some more shotguns? We only have the one, and if they should come back here..."

Pap laughed and said, "The more you poke at a turd, Esker, the louder it stinks."

He left the porch to refill his pipe. The summer's tobacco had been of good quality, and he smoked more of it than had been his previous habit. He lit his pipe and puffed until he produced a long retching cough. He resumed his seat.

"Our sentiments about slavery and particularly Mr. Lincoln will stay here at home or at our church. We will mind our own particulars, and I expect others shall do the same."

Social life on the porch dwindled as the weather turned cold and dry. Pap called it, "an anxious –making kind of dry."

By mid-February, a little rain fell, and Pap's countenance brightened some. The wheat was almost knee high, and looked like it would make a good crop. He and Esker were in the field, examining it, when a neighbor rode up at a gallop. His name was Bill and he had few teeth, and his expression indicated he had distressing news.

"Well, it's done," he said, and dismounted.

"What is 'done', Bill?" said Pap. Esker moved close so he could hear.

"Texas is secesh, like the rest of them idjits," said Bill. "Voted one hunert sixty-six to eight. Governor Houston is right peaked about it." He studied the ground for a moment and said, "I reckon he is real drunk right about now. I think I may go do the same."

"Who told you this?" said Pap, smiling. "It does not surprise me, but there is always one rumor and then another these days, you know."

Bill reached into his saddle bag and held out a newspaper. "Right here," he pointed.

Pap turned the paper over and read the banner. "The Marshall Texas Republican!!" he sneered. "You read this thing, Bill?" he grinned. "I thought this paper was only for secessionists and similar species of great apes."

Bill snatched his paper back. "Well, ye can think what you want, I suppose," his feelings were a little bruised, "but I am pullin' out and headed for Kansas, and maybe on to Illinois from there." He mounted his horse. "I ain't goin' to let this thing turn ugly before I get me and mine out. I reckon you might want to do likewise." He turned and cantered off.

Pap smiled at Esker. "Do not worry, Esker. Any little wind can blow the simple minded, and I fear Bill is one of them." He pulled up a wheat plant and shook the soil off its roots. "These roots are deep," he said. "It will take a bigger wind than this to move it."

The wheat was well up in April, and though it had turned dry again, the grain was forming. Pap was sowing corn with his stick and Esker was cultivating with the mule when they heard distant gunfire. It continued sporadically most of the morning, moving from river bottom to hilltop. Pap had finally become concerned enough to fetch his shotgun, and was walking back to the field when the Red Feathers rode up, whooping and shooting into the air.

"Well, look at you two ladies, just piddlin' about without a care," said the fat bearded man. "I suppose you have not heard the news." The five riders snickered and punched each other.

"No. What be the news, Orvis?" said Pap. He knew the fat man as the pugnacious child of a farmer on the Sabine. "It has been some years since I have seen you. How is your family?"

Orvis's smile faded. "My family is no concern to you, Lincolnite. We come to tell you that we got a war. Some Union fort just surrendered to the Confederacy at Charleston." This statement elicited more whoops and gunfire. "I suggest it is time for you to pull out of Texas and head home."

"Well, dear me, Orvis. Texas is my home," said Pap. "I have crops in the ground, and have three sons born here. I have not

7

hidden my sentiments, and I am no spy, nor are my boys. We will just tend our farm, and leave the politics and war to the likes of you."

"You're either for us or against us," said a man with a runny nose. "There ain't no middle ground around here. Y'all get, or y'all can rot. We'll be glad either way."

The horsemen then rode into the field and trampled the wheat. Orvis turned to Pap and said,

"We will look in on ye in a while. You'd best be gone."

May came in dry. The wheat which looked promising but trampled in April withered, and little of the corn sprouted. By the beginning of August, the black clay fields were hard as slab rock, and whirlwinds picked up dust and dropped it on the withered leaves of the trees. Curious, Esker dug a hole in the ruined corn field to look for moisture, but the soil was bone dry at three feet, where he gave up. Maw's vegetable garden was supplemented with buckets of well water, but even then, it wilted by the end of each hot day. Esker and his brothers spent more time in the river bottoms hunting. Surprisingly, the deer which had disappeared years ago reappeared in the woods along the river. The drought had driven them beyond their usual ranges and they were sometimes abroad even in the daytime seeking browse.

Pap and his cronies occupied the porch most afternoons and well into the night. They were scared. Several men and their families had taken the old Republic of Texas road north and east, and had left the state. Others were hanging on in hopes the storm would soon blow over. News print had become a scarce commodity. The Texas Republican, now the only paper available, printed a mere issue per month. The old men smoked and listened as Pap read an article aloud. He folded the paper and shook his head.

"Well, gentlemen. This here battle at Manassas does not bode well. General McDowell sounds like a lost cause, if you ask me," said Pap.

"Aye, Mr. Doyle, it appears to me that the rebels have too many graduates of that West Point school. They got all the best generals," said a fat man who sat on the steps below the porch. He stood and pointed his pipe stem at Pap. "They're mean, too. My Lord, all those ladies, and senators in their carriages had to witness that. All that rebel whoopin' and hollerin'. Musta scared 'em right outa their breeches."

The others smoked and gazed on the dusty floor in silence. "I will tell you what determined the outcome of this battle," said Pap. "The Union does not want a war. We are no cowards, but there ain't heart in it. The politicians know much bloodshed will divide this country forever. The South, though. The South wants the blood. It wants a war, not just the generals, but right down to the very soldier who shoulders a musket."

The drought persisted into the fall, and food became even scarcer. The tinder-dry grass carried fire through the prairies which worked their way into the woods where they burned for days. One evening, Esker stood on the front step admiring the peculiar quality of the smoky light at sunset.

"It is going to be a hard winter, Esker," said Pap. "I dreamt last night that I arose from my bed and wandered the house. The roof was burned off, and snow was on the floor and chairs.

Your brothers and your Maw sat, white as ghosts around the supper table with nary a crumb to eat."

"Where was I, Pap?" said Esker.

Pap put his hand on Esker's shoulder. "Well, I don't know," he smiled. "Perhaps you was gone off eatin' a beefsteak somewheres."

CHAPTER 2

The saloon sat at the edge of the Cowleech Fork of the Sabine River. The river bank had eroded so that the building's northeast corner dangled off the edge of a twenty foot drop. A hole had been poked through its floor so that the clientele could conveniently relieve themselves into the river below without leaving the building. It was a log construction, with un-chinked gaps large enough for a man outside to stick his head through, though that was inadvisable as the saloon's patrons were easily startled and rough in nature. It was a cold December, and the roaring fire in the fireplace did little to hold warmth against the wind which blew unimpeded through the gaps. A half dozen boys and men hunkered around a table and argued.

"Hunt County Vigilance Committee don't suit the nature of the enterprise," said one wearing a red feather in his hat band. He paused to stem the flow of snot from his nose with a sleeve which looked like it had been used for little else. "Hell, them boys in Missouri refer to themselves as Bushwhackers and such. We need dangerous-soundin' names like that."

Orvis Peck adjusted the big brass pistol in his belt so the hammer would not poke his fat belly. He took off his hat and stroked the red feather thoughtfully.

"We want to do this right and official," he said. "Names like that have the ring of banditry instead of right minded partisans." The crowd grumbled, though most agreed. "We'll call ourselves the Black Soil Partisans. How does that suit?"

"Suits me to the ground and back, Orvis," said a hairy man standing by a wide pine board that passed for the bar. He wore greasy buckskin breeches and had a greasy graying beard which hung to his waist. "Names are good and fine as far as it goes, but they mean nothin' if there is not doins' to go with 'em. The point bein' that you boys have done little other than to wear red feathers in your hats and prance around saying rude things to a few farmers."

The man with the runny nose was offended, but when he jumped to his feet, knocking over his chair, Orvis Peck grabbed his arm and sat him down.

"Elbert's not far off the mark, Peevis. Our rights as white men are drying up faster than mud in a hogwallow, and it is hard to know the right thing to do. Much of the farmers in the north counties are Lincolnites and abolitionist, and it is about clear that they will not leave on account of our askin' them to."

Elbert dragged a stool to the table and sat. He looked over his shoulder, scouting for eavesdroppers. He spoke low.

"Boys, there is a Methodist preacher, a circuit rider, who holds church up on the South Sulphur every other month. He is preachin' abolition to that bunch of subjects of King Lincoln. He don't keep a pet nigra with him like some do, but he got a Injun. Some boy. Looks like a school teacher." His audience snickered. "Reckon the best way to get our meaning clear is to get rid of 'em both. Do it where those Yankees can see it. They'll get the meaning. I'll vow it shall not be long before all of them are gallopin' for Indian Territory. Most won't make it that far."

CHAPTER 3

Church was bi-monthly, as long as the roads were dry enough to get there. In wet weather, the sticky black clay clung to the wheels of wagons and the feet of pedestrians to the extent that travel was almost impossible. Even a trip to the barn or privy resulted in the adhesion of ten or more pounds of black mud to the soles of shoes. But the weather had continued cold and dry. Christmas was approaching which made Maw even more determined to attend church and expunge sin from her boys and husband. In summer, most of the family bathed the night before church, though winter bathing was frowned on as an avenue for disease, especially consumption. As a result, only the necks and ears and faces of Poochy and Pie were scrubbed until they looked bloody, but Esker, being the oldest, was left to conduct his own ablutions.

The church was clapboard, and like the un-chinked log saloon on the Sabine, lacked battens to keep the wind out. The land it occupied was donated by the Doyles, who selected a part of their woodlot which had tall old post oaks with little scrub beneath. It was as pretty a site for a church as anyone had seen, but it was resented by some who thought the property had been given to curry community admiration and to keep the Doyles' trip to church a short one. Their cabin was only a quarter mile away.

The sun shone through the bare branches of the oaks the Sunday before Christmas, and the five Doyles approached the church on foot. Pastor Simmons stood at the door of the church and greeted the entering congregation. He was tall and lanky, and his thin hair stood out over his ears like horns.

Esker had read some Washington Irving, and he thought his description of Ichabod Crane came as close to describing Pastor Simmons as one could come. Esker thought he was a good man, if a little over-zealous. He condemned anyone who did not hold his views on God's grace and Christian living, or slavery. Most Texans would hold fast to the first two, but could not abide his viewpoint on the third.

The congregation, consisting of neighbors mostly known to the Doyles, milled around the church admiring new babies, discussing the drought, and eyeballing each other's Sunday clothes. Two tall windows, one behind the pulpit and one on the east wall lit the chapel so that clouds of dust motes sparkled in the shafts of sunlight. The room smelled of wool and tobacco and dirt, which was what most of the males in the congregation wore. Pastor Simmons mounted the pulpit and offered an opening invocation. A young, dark-skinned man sat behind and to the Pastor's right side. His black hair was cut short, but stood on end in such a way to create a halo around his head. He was simply dressed and wore glasses. When the Pastor finished and a hymn was sung by the gathering forcefully, if not well, the young man took the pulpit to read a lesson from the Bible. It was from Exodus, in which God threatened to kill anyone that "stealeth a man and selleth him." He did not stumble over any words, and read with a tenor and cadence surpassing the ability of the most well-read of the congregation. Esker was transfixed with admiration.

Maw bent to Esker's ear and whispered, "So well spoken, and an Indian!"

Esker had never really known an Indian. There were a few Shawnee who lived in the south part of the county, but he had

14

only seen them a few times. They wore blankets and braids and had little to say.

When the young man had finished, Pastor Simmons returned to the pulpit for the sermon. He fetched his glasses which were connected to a vest buttonhole by a little silver chain and perched them on the end of his nose, which was sharp and substantial.

"Permit me to read from our founder, John Wesley." He began. "Give Liberty to whom Liberty is due, that is, every child of man, to every partaker of human nature. Let none serve you but by his own act and deed, by his own voluntary action. Away with all whips, all chains, all compulsion. Be gentle toward all men; and see that you invariably do with everyone as you would he should be done unto you."

Pastor Simmons warned of the conflict between the states, which to him seemed inevitable and marvelous, but to Esker was confusing and fearful. Why was it, he thought, that he knew no one who owned slaves, and he knew no one who knew anyone who owned slaves, though many strongly favored fighting for the right.

The service ended with an ardent prayer for the end of the drought, and the congregation filed out.

The Pastor and his protégé, who was named Andrew Jackson, stayed the night with the Doyles. The older men sat on the porch and discussed the news of the most recent battles, and worried over the vigilantes. Occasionally, one or two would stand and peer down the road. The sound of distant horse hooves silenced the gathering. Esker sat on the steps and listened. The old men were apprehensive. Finally, Maw's call to supper sent some of the old men hobbling home, and others scrambling for a seat at the table.

CHAPTER 4

Andrew Jackson had little to say. He sat between Poochy and Pie, and was intimidated by their flying hands and elbows, and as a result, got little of the food. He watched Pastor Simmons closely. The pastor had been his mentor, and Andrew thought, if not like a father perhaps an interested uncle. He had traveled from Kansas to the Indian Territory and then to Texas two years before.

Andrew Jackson, a Kickapoo, had been called Little Hand by his mother and father. He knew this because he had been ten years old when the Comanche had descended on his camp, killing all of the people there, including his family. He had hidden in the brush along the creek, and had escaped notice. The Comanche mutilated his mother's and father's corpses as he watched. They scalped and gutted them. All the lodges of the village were made of long grass and tree bark, and they burned quickly. The massacre did not take long. It was over in less than fifteen minutes, and then the Comanche were gone. His people were poor, and did not have many good horses to steal, but the Comanche took what few they had. They would have gladly made a gift of the horses, but for the Comanche, there was no glory in taking gifts.

Little Hand hid by the creek for almost three weeks before someone found him. He lived on grasshoppers and little fish he could catch with his hands. The corpses in his village made a bad smell, so he moved farther downstream. One day, a young Kaw man was hunting deer along the creek, and caught a glimpse of Little Hand hiding in some reeds. Little Hand thought the enemies had returned. The man saw the ruins of the village and the dead, and understood that Little Hand was hiding and afraid. He dismounted and, holding his bridle rope, signed that he was a friend and would not hurt him. Little Hand crawled out of the reeds, though he was hesitant to come close. The Kaw, whose name was Looks Twice, pulled some jerked meat from a pouch he wore on his belt. He knelt and held out the meat for Little Hand to take. Little Hand's hunger overcame his caution, and he accepted the food.

Looks Twice put Little Hand on his horse. He rode without knowing exactly what to do with him. His band was poor, and he could think of no one to adopt him. The whites had made a mission for the Indians. There were many boys there. It was called the Shawnee Methodist Mission but, besides Shawnee, there were many Delaware and a few Kickapoos there. At least someone would be able to talk to him, and maybe he would find another band to live with.

A white man with a hairy face cut Little Hand's hair to his scalp. Little Hand thought the man should kill him first before he scalped him, but he was no coward and did not cry out. He was given clothes to wear which itched and made him sweat. His clothes looked just like the clothes the other boys wore. He was marched into a tall brick building and directed to a bed which stood high above the floor and had no animal pelts to make it comfortable. He watched the other boys to see what they did, and imitated them. They took off the clothes which were all the same, and put on long white shirts which were all the same. Some knelt by their beds and muttered while others just climbed into theirs. He called out to them in Kickapoo, but they only looked at him. An older boy signed to him. He told him to open the box at the end of his bed. There was a long white shirt. He put it on and climbed into the bed which was so high off the ground.

The older boy signed "Go to sleep. Do not make any noise or there will be trouble. Do not speak Kickapoo, it makes the whites angry."

The lantern was blown out by an old white man who spoke harshly to them. All was quiet. Though Little Hand had lived three weeks near the destruction of his village and the death of his parents, he had not felt loneliness until now.

Pastor Simmons taught English and put most of the boys to sleep twice a day and three times on Sunday with morning and evening prayers and a long sermon. Only half the students were proficient enough in English to understand what all the talk was about. However, most of the boys were impressed by oratory and pageantry. Pastor Simmons wore special robes with pretty decorations woven into them, and he used a special voice when he talked. The house he spoke in was obviously a sacred place, and on Sundays, they were given extra food at a meal following the service. Little Hand was fascinated by him. Often, when Pastor Simmons wore the robes and spoke, he gazed upon what appeared to be a stack of animal skins. They were white, and rustled like leaves when he moved them. Little Hand guessed that the spirit of the animal skins told him what to say. He wanted to know what the skins knew, and the only way was to learn the language of the man wearing the special robes.

Little Hand grew into Andrew Jackson, the white name given him by the missionaries. He was always addressed by both names, and called himself such. There was greater dignity in a bigger name. He was an apt pupil and learned to speak English quickly. It was not long before he could read it as well. Pastor Simmons was so amazed by his aptitude that he began reading Pilgrim's Progress to him after class. He later loaned him three or four books at a time until his own library, which was large by frontier standards, was exhausted. By the time he was fourteen, he assisted the Pastor with services, and read the epistle before the sermon. He spent many hours with Simmons discussing books, the Christian life and the declining state of the world.

Over time, the declining state of the world worried the Pastor so much that Andrew Jackson could no longer engage him in lively discussion. Simmons had always been cheerful, but lately had avoided him. Jackson's parents had taught him it was rude to ask a person a direct question, unless it was about the weather or hunting or where they were going. He could not ask him about his emotional state without breaching etiquette.

One day, the Pastor asked the boy to accompany him on a walk along the river. It was late in May, and plums were in bloom. The air was sweet with their fragrance. It was the most pleasant day Andrew Jackson could remember, this being the end of a particularly harsh winter. The Pastor was quiet, until he cleared his throat and said,

"I am leaving Kansas." Andrew Jackson was shocked, though he said nothing.

"The border ruffians have sacked Lawrence, with much loss of property. The worst of it is that they destroyed the printing presses of the two newspapers there." He said this with grave solemnity, letting his words sink in. "When free thinkers can no longer freely speak truth without retribution, we are no longer Americans. They have taken our mission town as their capitol, as well, and it is time to leave. I will take our message to other territories." He sat down on a rock, took off his hat and ran his fingers through his thin hair. He was tired. "It has been a long time since I took on pastoral duties beyond the mission, but it is time to leave." They sat in silence for some time, watching the river.

Andrew Jackson said, "I will go with you." Pastor Simmons smiled and rested his hand on his shoulder.

CHAPTER 5

Pastor Simmons left the Doyles early the next morning. Mrs. Doyle had sacked him up the few biscuits Poochy and Pie had left from breakfast. He rode an old brown nag with his elbows sticking out at right angles to his body. Esker stifled a laugh as he watched him and again thought of Ichabod Crane. The Pastor had met the widow Cheek, who was close to his own age. She was large and a renowned cook. Despite Simmons's thin frame, he was famous for consuming large quantities of food. Mrs. Cheek had invited him to supper. Her cabin lay a half-day's ride downriver. Andrew Jackson was left to the curiosity of Poochy and Pie, who had never talked to an Indian, and asked all of the rude questions Jackson knew to avoid. However, he was amused by the younger boys, and relegated their rudeness to youth and ignorance. Later that day, Esker intended to take him hunting. He too, was curious and wanted to get to know him, but thought conversation might be easier when they were occupied shooting squirrels for dinner.

The day was bright and crisp, and Pastor Simmons did not miss the bitter cold and snow that Kansans sometimes suffered around Christmas. The road along the river was dry, the travel easy, and even a few birds sang. At noon, he led his mule down to the river to drink. He sat and ate his biscuits, then lay in the leaves to nap. Against his closed eyelids, he watched the flickering shadows the branches cast across the winter sky. A shadow blocked the sun. He opened his eyes, and was surprised by a grinning and bearded face looking down on him.

"May I have this dance?"

The man offered his hand to help him to his feet. He grabbed Simmons roughly by the arm and dragged him toward the road.

"Let me lead you out to the dance floor," the man chuckled.

On the road, a half dozen mounted men waited. They and the laughing, bearded man wore red feathers in their hats.

"Where is that Injun brat ye keep?" asked a man with a runny nose. Simmons did not answer.

Orvis observed, "Well, I guess his dance partner has disappointed him! He will just have to dance alone."

One of the men led Pastor Simmons's horse to the road, and positioned it under the great limb of an oak tree. A noose dangled above the horse. The men all acted as if this was a great prank. He was politely asked to mount.

Simmons reluctantly climbed into the saddle, and said, "I thought I was rid of you when I left Kansas. But men void of reason or morals are not peculiar to any particular place."

At that, the bearded man slapped the rump of the horse. Simmons kicked a few times, and then hung like a dead fish. The party rode away; leaving the Pastor dangling above the middle of the road.

Peevis snickered nervously, "Do you think we should clamber down in the brush and wait to see who comes along first? Just to see what they'll do?"

Orvis said, "No, I think it would be best to ride on and start lookin' for his congregation."

CHAPTER 6

Andrew Jackson carried the shotgun. Clouds suddenly moved in from the northwest and the smell of rain was in the air. The sky looked heavy. It was warm, though, and the river bottoms smelled of mold and dead leaves. Few squirrels showed themselves, though Jackson easily dropped those that did. Esker skinned the squirrels and loaded them into a sack.

After he had finished, Andrew Jackson asked, "Have you read John Bunyan? Pilgrim's Progress?" Esker replied that he had, but had not finished it nor cared for the portion he had read.

"I think of it often," said Jackson. "I admit it is a difficult book, but the story is about a journey and struggle with the spirit." Esker was not sure what he meant, and squinted at him suspiciously. "The old people told stories like it to the boys in my village," said Jackson. "Many of those were about long journeys, too, where a man learned from animals or spirits what he needed to know to get to the next place or survive what he would find there. The past years with the Pastor have reminded me of those stories and of Bunyan. There were hard times in Kansas, and a long trip here, but we arrived."

"Sometime, I hope you would tell me some of those Indian stories," said Esker.

Andrew Jackson shook his head, grinning. "I am not 'Indian'. I am Kickapoo. To say otherwise, is like calling all you white people Dutchmen or Irishmen, see?" Esker was not sure of the point, but nodded in agreement out of politeness.

"Why do people call you by both your names?" asked Esker. "It takes too much time, and it tangles my tongue if I have to get it out of my mouth quick."

Andrew Jackson laughed. "Well .... bigger names signify a bigger person, I suppose." He dug his toe into the dirt, and after some consideration, looked at Esker. "You can call me Jackson, if you wish. It was given me. I did not decide to be called so, nor did I in any way earn the name, so I reckon it does not matter much."

They were climbing out of the river bottom when they smelled the smoke. Once they broke through the brush and onto the open prairie, they could see the fire. A black column of smoke and sparks rose from the patch of woods surrounding the Doyle cabin. Esker's heart raced as he ran blindly up the river terraces. Greenbriers and little shrubs tore at his clothes. His mouth was dry from fear.

Beside the burning cabin stood an oak, where three figures slowly turned in the wind. It had suddenly become too silent. Esker's ears buzzed with it. He thought such violence needed to be accompanied with much sound. The only sound was the rolling of the fire, punctuated by muffled explosions of the few oil lamps inside the cabin, which was now engulfed in flame. His father and brothers were hanged, and Esker's mother had disappeared. Esker stood transfixed. Jackson pulled the skinning knife from Esker's belt and cut the men down. He put his ear to the mouth of each, but looked sorrowfully at Esker and shook his head.

"I have to find Pastor Simmons." He peered down the River road where Simmons had recently departed. The rain had begun in earnest, and the road would soon be muddy. "Are there any horses?" Esker was unable to speak, but pointed to the mule shed.

The stalls were untouched, and the unperturbed white mule nibbled grain happily. Jackson saddled the mule, while Esker searched for his mother. A shred of her white apron poked up through the black mud along a little trail which led from the back of the cabin to the creek below. He followed it until he found her in a dogwood thicket. Her splayed bare legs were so white they glowed in the rain and gloom. Her dress had been pulled over her head. As he wept, he wiped the blood from her face, and organized her clothing modestly. She had been clubbed to death with a pistol butt. Esker remembered the big brass pistol carried by the fat man with the red feather in his hat.

CHAPTER 7

Jackson found Esker sobbing by his mother's corpse. Esker could not catch his breath or speak for a few minutes. Jackson sat beside him, and placed a gentle hand on his back.

"Esker, we have to bury your folks," he said softly. "We have to get it done and be gone. Pastor Simmons has to be warned, and whoever did this may be looking for us, as well. We are in danger."

They hurriedly buried Esker's family in the dooryard, though Esker vowed to come back and make a better job of it. There were no markers, and the graves were not deep enough to keep varmints at bay. Esker mounted the mule behind Jackson. The old mare was accustomed to the harness; was infrequently ridden, and had never supported two riders. She danced a little, and slipped on the slick mud as she made her way down the river road. They feared meeting up with vigilantes, and frequently sought high ground to survey the area. When they made the summit of the first little hill, they could see many new columns of smoke rising from the burning cabins in the surrounding valley. The smoke was black against a gray sky, and the low clouds reflected the red and orange light of the flames.

"I've never seen anything that looked so much like hell," said Esker.

"I surmise that it is," said Jackson. He kicked the mule and they descended the little hill.

It was fully dark and raining hard when they found Pastor Simmons. It had turned cold as well, and both riders tucked their chins to their chests to stem the rivulets of rain which ran from their hat brims and down their shirts. Jackson's hat was knocked from his head by Pastor Simmons's feet. The impact caused the limp body to twist and swing, and the wet rope to grate against the tree limb.

They sat silently on the mule, peering into the darkness. They were not sure who or what it was they were seeing. Eventually, they dismounted. Jackson climbed the tree and the long limb and cut the rope. Pastor Simmons's corpse fell hard to the wet road. They dragged him down to the flats along the river, and as it was wet and the soil deep, managed to dig a deeper grave than they had managed for the Doyles.

They found an overhanging bank by the river, and built a fire. The rain continued well into the night. It was a long time until sleep overcame them. At sunrise the rain had ceased, but a fine mist fell. Jackson found Esker sitting by the remains of their fire.

Esker said, "I am sorry I had to see my brothers and my Paw hanged and dead. But to see my Maw in such a state and to know that those men outraged her is heavy on me, Jackson." Jackson patted Esker, but said nothing.

Esker stood and wiped his wet face with his sleeve.

"If I can, I will kill the men who did it."

CHAPTER 8

The snow started the day after Christmas. The burned out cabin was veiled; the blackened timbers hidden by the snow. The snow made it a little easier to look at thought Esker, who had returned with Jackson to re-inter his family. He found horse blankets in the mule shed, and wrapped the bodies tightly in them before he and Jackson placed them gently in their graves along the river. He stacked a few stones to mark the head of each, and said a prayer over them. When they were finished, they followed the road to Mrs. Cheek's house. She wept for several days on hearing of the massacre of the Doyles and the murder of Simmons. She was a Baptist, and Esker assumed her denomination had provided her some amnesty, as the Methodists were the only vocal abolitionists in the neighborhood. She had been passed over, just like one of the Hebrews in a biblical plague. However, she feared she might be discovered harboring the boys. She feared she would share the fate of the Doyles. The boys were secreted in the smokehouse, a few yards from her cabin. They could not keep a fire there for fear of arousing suspicion. It was snug enough, though, with the blankets and quilts provided by Mrs. Cheek.

Esker had become silent. His grief over the loss of his family, especially his mother, laid heavily on him. They sat in the dark of the smokehouse, lit only with a candle.

"I know what it is to lose one's family, Esker," said Jackson. "Mine were murdered, too." He reluctantly told Esker his history. The loss of his family was an old story, and no longer caused him much pain, but the loss of Pastor Simmons was fresh, and caused his voice to break.

"I reckon we are both alike in that way," said Esker. "We are both orphans, I suppose."

Though they sometimes escaped to the river bottoms to hunt, life cooped up in the smokehouse was tedious. They ignored hygiene, and, having no extra clothes, wore the same ones day and night. It was not long before they were infested with lice, which they raced by candle light across a tin plate. Jackson's were consistently faster.

"They appear to do better on Indian meat," said Esker.

"Just a higher grade of victual, I suppose," said Jackson.

They otherwise spent most of their time arguing the plan for their escape from Texas. They decided they would try to make the Indian Territory. Once there, they could plan the next leg of the trip, though getting through to Kansas meant the possibility of confronting Comanche, and going further east required them to pass through Missouri, which was in turmoil. They had heard of refugees from Texas being detained and sometimes hung by vigilantes there.

Once a month, Mrs. Cheek's brother, Edmund, brought her mail and such staples as she could not herself produce. She was his youngest sister. He performed little chores for her, and worried over her being alone in such uncertain times. He was a burly man in his fifties, with long gray hair and threatening eyebrows. He discovered the boys on his second visit. It was early spring, and he wanted to determine how the remaining meats hanging in the smokehouse had fared over winter. He opened the door and found the two asleep there instead. Edmund filled the doorway, and the boys were blinded by the light which streamed in around him. Esker was sure the

31

partisans had found them and he scrabbled at the walls for an exit. Edmund was outraged that they would put his sister in such jeopardy by even thinking of allowing her to harbor them. He dragged them by their shirt collars into the house. They sat meekly at the table while Mrs. Cheek stood in the corner by her cook stove, and wrung her dish rag. After the shouting was over, Jackson told him their plans to flee north as soon as possible. He softened a little.

"Well, boys," he grinned. "Do ye not know that Jeff Davis has done passed him a conscription law, and boys your age are his meat?" He chuckled. He was enjoying himself. "Do ye ken that you need a paper from the government just to cross a county line?" he said. He moved his chair closer and leaned in conspiratorially. "If you boys try to get to the Territory from here, you will be caught and conscripted, or hung just as quick. Militia is thick from Clarksville to Gainesville. There ain't no way outta here." He leaned back in his chair, and smirked. "If I were you, I would head west across the Brazos and out to the buffalo range and join a ranging company. You might have to flee some Comanches, but they won't hang you. They'll just eat yer guts if they can catch ye." This statement amused him so much, that he laughed until he coughed. Then he lost all trace of humor. He spoke slowly and hotly.

"You boys get outta here quick, or I will fetch the partisans on ye. They can hang you right here in the yard. We got no shortage of stout limbs about. It will be no inconvenience to me." The boys gathered the shotgun and the mule, and led the latter into the nearby river bottom. Once they were well concealed, they sat in the mud, dejected.

"What will it be, Esker?" said Jackson. "Are you for hangin' by the militia or for the Comanches eatin' our guts?"

"I don't know. He may be telling us lies about the route to the Indian Territory. I suppose we should ride north and find out what we can along the way. In either case, we are not provisioned for a long trip. We need food, and another mount if we can."

Jackson smiled. "We can be horse thieves since we are already guilty of treason, I guess. I suppose we should drift west of north. The man told us the militia was thick from Clarksville to Gainesville. We might slip around them to the west. At least let's make Fort Worth before we decide whether to jump left or press on. It's not far from either the Brazos or the Red."

CHAPTER 9

The head of the Sulphur lay at the top of a prairie hill. They had ridden tandem through woods and forest, when suddenly the trees ended. The green and brown and red prairie grass climbed all the way to the sky and back. It startled Esker, who was familiar with the little prairie openings in the woods of east Texas, but was new to grassland which reached for the horizon. Jackson stopped the mule, and dismounted.

"This place lets me breathe better."

He stretched his arms up toward the sky and took a deep breath. His mood was considerably improved. The day was bright with little white clouds which looked like flocks of sheep. Their shadows raced with the wind across the prairie, which rippled and sighed appreciatively as they passed. The grasses were interspersed with blue, white and yellow flowers. Their aspect made Esker feel hopeful, though a little disoriented.

"My Lord! Can you imagine how many cows or sheep a man could keep on this grass?" gasped Esker. "We could be rich men, Jackson."

"I was a rich boy, when I lived on land like this," he replied. "My people had more than they needed, most years. We were up to our elbows in buffalo fat sometimes. Those were greasy years." The thought of those good times made him a little sad. "I have been thinking that it might be good to kill me some Comanches." He narrowed his eyes at Esker, "That is if they

34

don't eat our guts first!" He laughed and slapped Esker on the shoulder, who did not see the humor.

The mule crested the big hill, which divided the Sulphur from the Trinity watershed. They saw a large cabin situated above a little creek, which hosted the few trees they could see. They stood watching for motion around it.

"Do you think we dare it?" asked Esker. There was no smoke rising from the chimney, though they could see some livestock and a horse grazing near the house.

"We need food. Either we can ask for it or steal it," said Jackson. "Let's find out which we'll do."

When they approached the cabin, they saw a man and woman of middle years loading a wagon. The man was bald and had chin whiskers. When they hailed him, he ran to the cabin and returned with a shotgun.

"What is your business, travelers?" When Esker attempted to dismount, the man discharged one of the two barrels of his gun into the sky. Esker quickly remounted. The man's accent was not east Texas and his flattened vowels sounded midwestern. Esker took a chance with the truth.

"Mister, we are fleeing a mob who don't want us in Texas. They killed my mother and father and my two brothers. We are just trying to make the Territory. My friend and me are seeking provision to hold us till we get somewheres." The man lowered the shotgun.

"Well..." he looked back to his wife who was hiding behind a post on the porch. "My wife and I are in the same fix, I fear. We were visited by those so-called Black Soil Partisans last night—the ones who wear the red feathers in their hats. They burned out our neighbors west of here, and then drove off most of our stock and threatened to hang us both if we were not departed by today."

"I am sorry for your troubles, sir," Jackson offered. "May we help you load your wagon?"

They spent the remainder of the morning loading furniture and goods onto the man's wagon. He was a Pennsylvanian named Clymer. As they worked, he told the boys he had built his place in the early '50s following a stint in California panning for gold. He had moderate success, and had acquired more than ten thousand acres on his return. He had also lost his scalp to some irritable Navajo who mistook him for Kit Carson.

"I was better looking then," he rubbed his scalp and laughed. "I thank you boys for your assistance," he said. "I would loan you a horse, but as you can see, this old nag is the only one left us. Let me provide you some parched corn and some bacon. That should keep you for a while."

"Are you going to try for the Territory?" asked Jackson.

Clymer said, "Yes, and you would be wise to not delay. The Partisans will be here shortly."

"We have not decided," said Esker. "We were told the militia was thick as dog hair along the Red between Gainesville and Clarksville. Jackson and me are going to try to drift west of Gainesville."

Clymer looked doubtful as he shook their hands farewell. "Well...watch the Comanches once you get west of the Brazos. They will eat a man's guts if they catches him."

CHAPTER 10

They traveled downhill a few miles toward a sizeable creek. Bur oaks and pecan trees lined its banks, and the temptation to eat some of the corn in the cool shade was irresistible. They would not risk a fire for the bacon, which was turning a little green anyway. The mule was worn and thin and needed the rest as well. She nibbled the thick wildrye and the boys ate the parched corn. It had been three days since they had eaten. Their last meal was a stringy little prairie chicken, which they had flushed at the edge of the Sulphur River bottoms. Their hunger was damped for the first time in almost a week. Esker spread the saddle blanket and dozed while Jackson searched the forest floor for pecans.

Esker was awakened by Orvis Peck, who kicked him in the ribs hard enough to roll him off the blanket.

"Well, little man. I looked for ye when I hung your paw and brothers. I wondered where you had run off to. I was right concerned, but now have I found you, here within your lovely little bower." He cocked his brass pistol and pushed the barrel into Esker's ear. "All is well that ends so, I suppose." He bared his tobacco-stained teeth. "Where is that little bastard of a Injun you been ridin' with?" he glanced around. "I suppose he will have his turn later."

Peck's feathered hat and his right ear landed on Esker's chest, even before he heard the report of the shotgun. Peck rolled onto Esker, then sat up, dazed. The bird shot was not enough to kill him. Esker picked up the ear and offered it to Peck.

"Mister? I believe this is your ear."

Peck, astonished, accepted it as he felt the side of his head where his ear had lately resided. Peck's pistol lay next to Esker, who picked it up and stood beside Jackson. Peck slowly gained his feet. He was unsteady, but pulled a long knife from his boot, while he stanched his bleeding head with a dirty bandana in his free hand.

"I'm gonna gut both of you before I kill ye. My posse is right behind, and they have surely heard the report of your shotgun," he snarled.

"Then I guess it won't hurt much if they hear two shots."

Esker pulled the trigger on the big brass pistol. The shot hit Peck in the throat, and he fell to his knees gargling blood. Esker stepped to Peck's side.

"Or three, I suppose."

The third shot took off the top of Peck's head and his struggle ceased. Esker was dazed, but rolled Peck over and unbuckled his gun belt which had two loaded cylinders for the pistol, a Navy Colts. He rifled through his pockets and found a clasp knife, percussion caps, chewing tobacco, twenty dollars in Mexican silver, and enough dirt to start a small garden.

"I guess we can ride separate, now," whispered Jackson, whose ears still rang from shock and gun fire.

He rifled through Peck's saddle bags taking inventory, and laid the contents on the ground. There was coffee, gun powder, primers, bullets and a bible, but no food. He pulled a rifle from the saddle scabbard. It was a Sharp's breech loader.

The butt had been broken, but repaired with rawhide and brass tacks. It was serviceable. He opened the breech and looked down the barrel. It was a prize, especially since it would provide meat for the journey. He quickly repacked the contents. Esker saddled the mule, and Jackson mounted Peck's horse, a roan mare which was restive following all of the noise.

"Well, I suppose we are rich now, Esker."

Esker did not hear him. "Let's go before the posse catches up. We are murderers along with bein' traitors." He turned to Jackson, his eyes filled. "Well, at least we earned our hangin' now."

CHAPTER 11

Peck's partisans had not heard the gunshots since they were preoccupied with shooting the air and whooping while they looted Clymer's cabin, then set it afire. They had found a jug of tolerably good whiskey, and after they squabbled over it, passed it around a campfire they had built from Clymer's fence. It was sundown before Jimmy Peevis set down the bottle, wiped his nose on his sleeve, and looked puzzled. He walked beyond the firelight and looked northwest, the direction Peck had ridden that afternoon, following the trail of the escaped Unionist boys. Edmund Winkler, the brother of the Widow Cheek, had reported their direction of travel the day before. Peevis supposed Peck had tracked them till dark, and would be back in the morning with some trophies—some ears or a scalp or two, perhaps.

When Peck did not appear by noon the following day, Peevis called a meeting of the partisans. About half had left for home, dissipated by the night of carousing and house burning. The six remaining men were in poor shape as well. They mounted and reluctantly trailed Peck to the creek bottoms, where they found what remained of him. The buzzards were thick when they rode in, and coyotes had been at the corpse as well.

"I'd say Orvis is a bit scattered about," said Peevis, whose night of whiskey was not helping him keep his vomit down. He salivated so much he could barely speak. "You fellers gather him as best you can, and I reckon I will dig him a grave," he gurgled.

The remainder of the afternoon they argued about pursuing Peck's killers. Peevis was determined that they should pursue them; others were in favor of returning home.

"Peck was plenty mean," said one of the older men who frequently disagreed with Peevis. "Those two boys weren't the ones who done this. Hell, they're just boys, and Yankees to boot. It must have been a whole party of Unionists, or maybe Injuns." He spat tobacco juice in the little fire they had made to cook bacon. He looked Peevis in the eye. "I am goin' back. If you want to put together another, bigger expedition, you let me know. I recommend the rest of ya do the same." One by one, the partisans quietly mounted their horses and mules and rode out of camp.

Peevis hollered, "By God, if y'all ain't a sight." He wanted to say more, but could not find the words. "Shit," he said, and flopped down on a stump by the fire.

CHAPTER 12

The sun was setting by the time they found the old Republic road, which ran from Clarksville southwest to the Trinity River. The road could be followed by a blind man. It was a three hundred feet wide trail of ruts and mud, made broad by wagons avoiding ruts and mud left by others over the past twenty five years. The boys made camp in a ravine near the road, but far enough away to escape detection. The Republic road was the easiest route out from northeast Texas, and they assumed the most heavily patrolled by the militias. Their hobbled mule and horse grazed even further from the road. Clymer's gift of parched corn had been eaten. They decided to risk a small fire to cook his bacon. Jackson had a small, ornate pouch hidden beneath his shirt. He pulled from it a steel and flint and lit tinder. Esker was fascinated by the pouch which had floral designs embroidered on it.

"That is a nice gewgaw you got there," Esker said. "Where did you get it?"

"It was my father's. I've heard it called a strike-a-light pouch, but I can't remember the Kickapoo name for it." Once the fire was started, he pulled its cord over his head and handed it to Esker. "It was a great deal of effort to hide it from the missionaries," he said. "They would not let us keep anything from our old lives. I wrapped it in some rags and buried it. Dug it up and took it with me when the Pastor and I left Kansas."

"My, it is fancy. What kind of decoration is that?" said Esker.

"Porcupine quill. I think my mother made it."

"I've never seen a porcupine, though I have heard of them." He returned the bag to Jackson.

"It just reminds me that I am Kickapoo," said Jackson, running his fingers over the quill work. "I think that it is the intention of the mission schools to make us think we are white people, and forget we are regular people," said Jackson.

"Do you think you are a white man, Jackson?"

"No. But sometimes I fear that I am so infected by white men that I can no longer be Kickapoo."

"Infected?" said Esker. Jackson did not answer.

They were awakened in the morning by the sound of the tramping feet of men and horses and rattling tack. They peered over the edge of the ravine and discovered a column of federal soldiers marching northeast. Their blue uniforms were tattered and covered in dust. There were less than a dozen men. Most were unarmed, and all looked dejected. Esker, grinning, let out a whoop and scrambled up the bank, before Jackson could stop him. Esker ran toward the soldiers, shouting with a goofy smile on his face. Those few who were armed brandished rifles and pointed bayonets at him.

"Don't shoot!!" screamed Jackson. Now the rifles were pointed at him. "We are Unionists!! We are Unionists!!"

A young Lieutenant, mounted on a fine-looking horse, rode into the middle of the knot of soldiers. He was cleaner than the rest. Esker could tell, even at the distance of a few feet, that his fingernails were clean and trimmed.

"How do I know that you are not a spy?" the lieutenant demanded. "How do I know that you have not conspired with the damned vigilantes to impede us?" he sneered.

"No, Sir!!" replied Jackson, who had just arrived, out of breath. "We are pursued by a secessionist mob. We want to go with you. We will even join the Army if you wish," he said. The soldiers laughed.

"Ain't much of an army left to join," said a private. The Lieutenant glared at them. He was not pleased with the delay and ordered the march resumed.

"That goddamn traitor Twiggs has sent you to thwart us, and I shall not bear it." He spat a stream of tobacco juice at Jackson's feet and rode on.

They watched the column pass. An enlisted man paused and placed his hand on Esker's shoulder sympathetically.

"I am sorry boys. We been in the Confederate stockade at Camp Colorado for the last year. Been there ever since Twiggs surrendered the forts and McCullough took 'em. They finally let us go. We got some kinda paper of safe passage, but we been mobbed more than once by bushwhackers. The Lieutenant is right irritated. Besides," he motioned to two wagons following, "the Lieutenant and some of the boys got their wives with 'em. Most of the troops stuck with the rebs. Can you believe that? And now we done marched all the way, clear out on the upper Colorado River." He looked up the road and hoisted his haversack.

"It's this way, fellers. We are runnin' out of food, horseflesh and shoe leather. We can't feed you. You'd do best

45

to stick and hide out if you can. Maybe this little squall will blow over quick."

They watched the soldiers disappear in the distance.

"Do you think we could follow behind at some distance, Jackson?"

"I don't think that little officer will tolerate it," said Jackson. "Besides, I am not sure the militia will let them pass. There are not many of them, and only a few were armed."

"Well, I suppose we need to find Fort Worth, then," said Esker to himself. Jackson was already saddling his horse.

CHAPTER 13

They turned southwest, and paralleled the road a mile or so south of its route. They did not risk encounters with vigilantes or soldiers. They had no bona fides for travel. Bandits, too, had become a particular problem on the road in the past year. The prairie they traversed was vast, though broken by little creeks and streams. Though they saw few cabins and the land was largely unsettled, game was scarce. Buffalo had disappeared from the clay prairies almost twenty years before. The antelope too, had all but vanished. They occasionally saw the flash of white from the rump of a white tailed deer, but had never come close to them. Starvation was becoming a serious concern. They decided to keep the rifle loaded in case they encountered larger game. Neither of them had much experience with rifles, only the occasional use of a shotgun, which they carried as well, though they had expended the remaining bird shot on Orvis Peck. Jackson gathered the few prepared paper cartridges and levered open the breech of the rifle. The cartridges were slightly damp, and he had trouble inserting one into the breech. The paper tore. Esker watched, biting his lip.

"Well..." he said. "We don't want to waste those. If it rides in the breech the next day or two, perhaps it will dry out. As long as it don't rain, I guess."

Early the next day, as they approached the forest along the East Fork of the Trinity a small herd of deer browsed the scrim of brush at the forest's edge. The deer stopped eating and gazed at them, but apparently saw the horses but not their riders. Jackson slowly pulled the rifle from its scabbard and aimed carefully. He squeezed the trigger. Thunder and lightning jumped from the barrel and he departed the saddle in the opposite direction. The deer fled, unharmed. He sat in the weeds for a moment, then gathered his reins.

"At least the horse did not bolt," he said as he rubbed his hind quarters.

The forest along the river was thick. Mosquitoes swarmed around the green ash swamps. The aerial roots of the trees were at such height to indicate the water had been commonly higher. Crowfoot sedge and tough grasses grew beneath them. The spring had been a dry one, and so far they had traveled dry. They found a little rise in the middle of the forest where a single bur oak grew, and the brush was sparse. They decided to camp and hunt for food. They picketed their horses in a dry loblolly. Esker took the loaded Sharps and Jackson carried the pistol.

"Even if we find a recent carcass of a deer, I would not turn my nose up," said Jackson.

Esker looked a little green, and said, "I believe I will eat grass first." They had scrambled about a mile through thickets when the mosquitoes became so thick that they were driven from the forest and onto the prairie above. It was dotted with blue flowers. When Jackson saw them, his face lit up.

"Breadroot!!" he shouted. "My mother dug these up with a stick. They are fine victuals."

They cut sticks and spent several hours digging up the thick pulpy roots attached to a plant which reminded Esker of a bean. Esker took his shirt off and made a pack to carry the roots back to their camp. They built a fire, and, burning it down to coals, baked them. Jackson relished them, and talked excitedly with his mouth full, remembering the way his mother had prepared them, and extolling their virtues in flavor and nutrition. Esker was able to swallow the tubers, which seemed to expand in his mouth as he chewed, but he did not care for the flavor. They seemed to expand in his stomach as well. When they had eaten their fill, they built a smoky fire to keep the mosquitoes at bay and rolled into their saddle blankets to sleep. Esker's belly continued to bloat until he could stand it no longer and ran for the brush. He was explosively ill most of the night. In the morning, Jackson nudged him awake with the toe of his boot.

"I guess breadroot is just good for us Indians," he laughed. "But not all," he consoled. "My mother's brother, we called Duck. That was not his real name, but we called him so because his hind quarters spoke like a duck when he ate it."

CHAPTER 14

They crossed the East Fork at a ford which had been a buffalo crossing. It had been used by wagons for so many years, the approaches on both sides of the river were sunken far below the grade of the surrounding forest. Two or three old and rotten wagon boxes were stranded in the mud or scattered along the shores, showing that crossing this point was not always an easy matter. Esker had recovered from the breadroot, and both were ravenously hungry. They threw their shoes on the bank and waded into the water in search of anything edible. Esker flipped rocks until he had collected enough crawfish to make a small meal for the two of them. Jackson found a few mussels as well. Lacking cooking utensils, they threw the viands on the coals of a hastily constructed little fire, then, dividing them equally, mashed the food into their mouths as rapidly as possible.

By early afternoon, they emerged from the forest and onto the prairie, which was different than the ground they had trod before. As far as they could see across the level ground little mounds and basins the size and depth of bathtubs made riding difficult. Esker's father had called such hogwallow prairie, though he said the ground itself created the depressions. Esker's mule picked its way through easily enough, but Jackson's horse needed to think about each step. Progress was slow, and Esker was often more than a quarter-mile ahead.

Jackson called to Esker, and pointed with his chin to the northwest. The sky was black and green along the horizon, and thunder muttered in the distance. The air hung still and muggy, and the birds had stopped singing. Esker slowed his mule and let his friend's prissy mare catch up. There was no shelter in sight.

"Well…" sighed Esker, looking around. "Looks as though we are gonna get our fancy beaver hats wet, Jackson."

Jackson smiled weakly. Their hats were old sweat stained felts which had holes in the crowns and the brims looked like the goats had been at them.

"Yes. I left my good parasol at home, too," he said.

A big gust of wind preceded the storm. It made a wave through the grasses as they bent before it. They could see the wave approaching from almost a mile away. When the wind hit them, their hats took off like wild geese and disappeared into the sky. The first hailstones were no larger than pennies, but within seconds were as large as silver dollars. They climbed under their mounts, who were pelted by the hailstones and flinching. They moved around so much, they were little protection. The boys took the saddles off and covered their heads with them. They sat in the rain and hail, and held onto their reins as best they could. The hail stopped and a deluge followed. Lightning struck nearby and threw thick black clods into the air. They sat dejected in the sopping hogwallows and waited.

The storm passed in less than an hour. They saddled their horses and resumed the trek. Now the hogwallows were brimming with water, and toads and frogs alternately sang and screamed as they picked their way through the prairie.

CHAPTER 15

After two days, they exited the hogwallow prairie, and climbed a limestone ridge bearing southwest. The Republic Road followed the ridge for almost fifty miles. It had shallow chalky soil, was well used and a luxury after stumbling through the wet clay. After several hours, and late in the day, they encountered an intersection. A second, less worn trail bore due north. A small, hand lettered wood sign indicated "Dallas," with a north-pointing arrow scratched into it, which looked like an afterthought.

"I don't have business to attend in Dallas," said Esker. "I heard there are troops bein' mustered there, besides. I judge it would be best to drop south of the road again for a while."

Far to the west, they could see forest. Against the prairie, it looked like the shore of a distant continent. Jackson agreed to the plan, though departing the road put them on the rough clay prairies again. After a full day of hard travel, they camped on the edge of the forest which cloaked the main trunk of the Trinity River. The woods were bigger than any they had seen since leaving east Texas. Pecan, elm, and red oak trees towered over the forest floor, which was swept clean of brush and deadfalls by frequent floods. They were again without food, and on the verge of starvation. They had seen no game, but Jackson pulled the rifle from its scabbard, and peered down its breech. He replaced a torn cartridge and slipped the few remaining into his pocket.

"I am going to find food. I don't care what it is. I am going to eat it," said Jackson.

He hoped to kill a deer, but all the game trails were stale. There was no fresh sign. In a clearing, he found scattered wild onions. He pulled up a dozen and pressed half of them on Esker, who recognized them immediately and ate them dirt, leaves and all.

"Better than that breadroot, I'd say." He belched from his empty stomach. "What's for dessert?"

The game trail led to a small creek, which meandered through the forest. The water in the creek deepened, and terminated at an old beaver pond. The beaver had long since been trapped out, but the dam held enough water to grow duck potatoes, another alien food for Esker. Nevertheless, he took off his shirt and stuffed the wet tubers in.

"These just look like those breadroots, but I'll eat about anything that presents itself at this point," he said.

They made a fire by the pond and roasted them. Jackson showed Esker how to peel them. The potatoes were not a food which could be eaten quickly, and by the time they finished, the sun had begun to set.

"We need to get back to the horses, Mr. Jackson," said Esker as he saw the last light touching the canopy of trees. They packed up the rifle and the few remaining potatoes. When they were a few yards up the trail, there came crashing through the underbrush a large black hog. Esker had thought it a bear at first, and had begun climbing a tree. Jackson leveled his rifle and fired just as the pig, a large, old and pugnacious sow, entered the trail. The lucky shot caught the sow just behind her right ear. She fell to her left side and slid a few feet before coming to a stop at Jackson's feet. He turned to Esker with his mouth wide open in surprise.

He hooted, "Now, Esker, I know that you would as soon pick her up like a slice of watermelon, and eat her raw, but we have some butchering to do first." Esker was so excited he was speechless. Instead of dragging the carcass back to camp, he brought their mounts to the carcass. Jackson was adept at dressing game, and was already cutting a side of bacon when Esker rode up on the mare with the mule in tow.

Jackson continued his butchering while Esker prepared a fire. He made a rack of green sticks and placed the side of bacon above the coals. The fat ran into the fire and smelled so delicious that Esker drooled on his shirt. He repeatedly ran his forearm across his mouth to stem the flow. Jackson was little better off and insisted Esker cut a little burned corner as a sample before the side was entirely done. They were so enthralled they did not hear Allanson Dowdy, who stepped out of the brush behind them.

"You boys are eatin' my sow, I guess. Is she tasty?" He leveled his shotgun at them. Esker and Jackson turned, startled.

Esker raised his hands and said, "Mister, that hog was charging us. We shot her defending our lives." Dowdy picked up the hog's head and examined the ears.

"Got two notches on the left ear," he sighed, resigned. "Her name was Wilhelmina. I named her after my deceased wife. She wasn't attacking you son, she just thought you might feed her. She liked her little goodies. Hell, a corn dodger or two would do. She liked to have her ears scratched, too."

"We regret killing your hog, sir," said Jackson. "We have been without food for a long time, but we killed her because it appeared she might eat us."

Esker said, "I have some money. We can pay for her." Dowdy had a long, grizzled beard which he picked at as he thought.

"I don't need money. I've sufficient. You boys can keep a side of bacon and the hocks, I reckon, but you will work for me for a day to make up for the loss of my pet. I might have eaten her myself eventually, but I enjoyed scratchin' her ears of an evenin'."

Allanson Dowdy ran a ferry on the Trinity River about twenty miles below Dallas. There was a tidy cabin, a small store and a large raft. The latter was constructed of four cottonwood logs with planks lashed between them. It was sufficient to carry a single wagon and team, or four horses and riders. They found Dowdy the following day.

"I am pleased that you come. Now I know you both are gentlemen who honor your debts," he said.

He put them to work repairing and replacing lashings on the raft. At noon, he beckoned them to join him under the shade of his porch, and gave them bread and bacon. He told them he had come to Texas in the 1830's and had served in the revolution. He was thinking of closing the ferry to join the Confederate army, now mustering in Dallas.

"You boys are not too young to do the same," he looked at them carefully. "But that runs against your sentiments, I surmise." Esker stood, ready to run at the first sign that

Dowdy would reach for his shotgun, which was always at hand.

"Keep your seat, young man," Dowdy smiled and passed a hand over his mouth. "My sentiments do not run too much contrary to your own. I am an Illinois man, but I have been with Texas so long, I see it as my duty to join up. Texas is my country, you see, but I don't care much for the cause. I will do what I can, and if I can." Esker sat down, and Jackson nervously picked at the loose threads on his breeches.

Dowdy explained, "You men were traveling far from the road. You don't have the mean look of outlaws, so I naturally assumed you were fleeing those vigilantes to the east. We have not had trouble as such here, but we have heard about the depredations of several bunches toward the Sabine River." He shook his head sadly and said, "I suppose you will try to make the Territory, but I recommend against it. Even if you leave here with your tail feathers all aflame and get to the Red in a week, they will be watching. Gainesville, there on the river, is mighty stirred up and is lookin' for Union spies along with anyone else they can catch and hang. In the last month they rounded up over forty men and boys suspected of nothin' more than sympathizing with the Union. They hanged ever last one. I think some were hanged to settle personal scores, if you want to know what I think. On the other hand, the Comanche are thick north of that part of the Red. They are crossin' almost daily to raid along the edge of the Cross Timbers. You would be better off crossing the middle Brazos and laying low out on the range till this squabble settles down."

Esker still had Orvis Peck's money, and he bought ammunition, a frying pan, flour, salt pork, coffee, salt and canned tomatoes. They bought waxed canvas tarps for protection against the rain as well as two hats replacing those lost to the wind in the prairie storm. Dowdy watched them pack their goods.

"I am going to give you each a pair of drawers and a suit of clothes," he said. "I was distracted by the lice crawlin' on you while we were havin' an otherwise pleasant conversation. Throw them lousy clothes in a pile yonder in the yard and I will burn them later."

So equipped, they felt confident they were prepared for a long expedition. Dowdy ferried them across the river, and shook their hands solemnly when they reached the western shore.

"You fellers beware, and I hope that I shan't see you on the opposite side of the battle ground," he said, and hauled his ferry back to the other side.

CHAPTER 16

The country immediately west of the Trinity turned to clay prairie again, but with fewer hogwallows than they had encountered on the east side. They passed through the country quickly. On the morning of the second day, they entered a savanna of oak trees and shade which Esker greatly admired. He had grown up with towering post oaks in east Texas, but these trees were short and gnarled, with thick boles and sparse branches. The trees' canopies, however, were sufficiently high, and their spacing scattered so to make travel through them easy. They had salted the side of bacon and the hocks before leaving Dowdy's ferry, but they had already begun to stink in the saddle bag. They decided to camp among the oaks and eat as much of the pork as they could before it turned entirely.

Esker opened the saddle bag containing the pork and grimaced. "That sow has a whang to her. I reckon we can cut out the worst parts."

There was much tall dry grass beneath the oaks, mostly bluestems, but one Jackson knew as purpletop grew thick as well. It was green and in flower, and made the woods smell like plums. They managed a little fire and cooked half of the bacon. When they had finished eating, they sat in the shade and sucked pork grease from their fingers.

"Livin' like kings, I'd say," said Jackson.

"Yessir. Like kings." Esker shifted his seat and looked at Jackson. "A few days ago, you told me that you had been 'infected' by white men. Are you sick, Jackson?"

"No, Esker." He broke a twig from a low hanging branch and idly picked his teeth. "Being Kickapoo is more than just being born into the people. Most boys spend the better part of their youth learning how to live like one. I was interrupted, I suppose, and taught to be white. They tried to cut the Indian out of me. But I think you have to cut mighty deep to get it all." He leaned toward Esker and said, "Please understand. I miss Pastor Simmons. He was a good man. But the more time passes without him, the more I feel like myself." He grinned at Esker and threw his chewed up twig at him. "But telling you about this is about as white as anything I have done for some time."

Esker was confused, but smiled. "Well, bein' a white man ain't all bad. Not all the white men are bad, anyway. You are the only Indian I have knowed, so I have little to judge your character by."

Wind kicked up sparks from the cook fire. It started a little blaze in the grass which they whacked fiercely with their saddle blankets, but their efforts only spread it. When the flames caught the lower branches of the oaks, they determined it was time to leave, since the smoke might lead to their detection.

They passed through the woods within a few hours, and emerged on their west side. Before them lay an expanse of prairie unlike either had seen. The trees ended abruptly behind them, and in front lay grassland void of even a shrub to break the view. They were now far north and west of the road, and had lost the trail from the ferry. They decided to follow a creek until it met with the West Fork of the Trinity and follow it upstream until they found Fort Worth. It was not long, however, before they intersected a wide road bearing generally west. They followed it to its junction with the river where four freight wagons labored to cross a shallow ford. They decided to rest beneath a tree on the river bank and allow their horses to graze until the freighters had passed. Each wagon had a team of six oxen, and the freighters cursed and hollered and cracked whips across their broad, struggling backs. Their loads were obviously heavy, and it took over an hour to get the four across and up the west bank. They were curious about the heavy cargo and the destination for the freight.

"What are you all haulin'!?" shouted Esker.

"Rock!!! Goddamn a rock!!" shouted a teamster.

Esker sat down with his back against a live oak. "We have to choose. Either North or West, Andrew Jackson," Esker said. "I suppose we have been told more than once that North is impassible, but you appear to need more evidence than I do."

Jackson apologized. "It occurred to me to go home. I have a grandmother who might still be around the Konza River. But I like the thought of shooting at some Comanche, too." He turned to Esker. "One more time. We will ask around one more time. Then decide." He pointed his chin at the last wagon climbing the bank and mounted the mare.

A mile from the crossing, the road climbed a steep bluff. At its top stood the village of Fort Worth and the foundation and the first few courses of a new, large stone building. The freighters were supervising a group of Negroes who slid large limestone blocks down ramps attached to the wagon beds. The rest of the town was made up of simple limestone buildings which were the remnants of the fort built in 1849, and abandoned a few years later; repurposed into houses and stores. There were a few log cabins and several buildings of milled lumber. The streets which divided both house and commercial lots were merely strips of mud and horse manure. Wagon traffic had further rutted and roiled the mud.

Most of the town's population stood in the street, crowded in front of a large frame building. Before them a woman, elevated on a platform and seated on a chair, held a baby to her bare breast. She was tied to the chair at her waist and her feet were bound. A sign attached to the platform described her as Anna Belle Langley, formerly a child of an influential family, and lately a Comanche Indian. Her uncle described her ordeal with the Comanche and her heroic rescue by the Texas Rangers. He said she did not speak much English anymore, and requested donations to help with her recovery and rehabilitation.

Jackson shouldered his way into the crowd so he could see her better. Her face was expressionless, but her blue eyes showed terrible sorrow. Her gaze was fixed on the prairie beyond the crowd, but Jackson momentarily caught her attention.

He signed, "It is a bad thing they do here to let white men stare at you." She signed with her free hand.

"I don't talk to Kickapoos," and she spat on him.

CHAPTER 17

Esker looked for someone away from the crowd, who they could question in private. Fort Worth was less than seventy miles south of Gainesville, with few settlements between. There were no Confederate troops or militia apparent, but their questions had to be carefully pitched to the right person in the right way.

An old man sat in the shade of a small motte of live oaks near the unfinished stone building. He swigged from a bottle, and made comments or shouted directions at the workers, who, if they had cared to hear him, could not, due to his distance and his slurred speech.

Esker said, "He might be good to sit with for a bit. We can ask him questions, and he looks drunk enough that he won't remember us tomorrow." Jackson agreed, but looked dubious.

"Well...A drunkard might be confused, but as they say, En Vino Veritas." Esker looked at him blankly.

He explained, "In Wine is Truth. It's Latin. It means drunkards tell the truth."

"Oh," said Esker, a little irritated that his friend liked to flaunt his superior education from time to time. "Well, let's us go talk to him."

The old man looked up at their approach and smiled his four teeth at them. "How do ye?" he asked.

"Tolerable well," smiled Esker. "May we sit with you?"

"Join me!" he said, and with a grandiose sweep of his arm, gestured to the rocky ground next to him. He looked at Jackson and wrinkled his nose as though he smelled something objectionable. "Are you a Injun?" Jackson nodded. "I hate Injuns, all kinds. You sit over there." He pointed to a patch of grassless ground a few feet away. It was beyond the shade. "Do you have any whiskey? I am pretty well out." He showed the little in the bottom of his bottle and drained it.

"No sir, we don't drink," replied Esker.

"More's the pity," said the old man. "I has sat right here for three days, watchin' those idjits build a stone courthouse the wrong way," he sneered. "The white men are worthless, and the nigras are worse!" He rifled through a tow sack and found a bottle with a dab of whiskey in its bottom. "I built all of those rock houses in the fort, ye know," he gestured to the scattered stone structures behind them. "Been there more 'an a decade. Will be there forever," he shook his head sadly. "I came here in '49 and mustered out when the fort was decommissioned, a big mistake, but nobody asked me." He squinted at the courthouse for a moment, then pointed a dirty finger at it. "A strong fart will blow that thing down, I vow."

"Well ... yessir. A strong fart should be avoided then, I'd say," said Esker thinking of a way to change the subject. "We came here to see if the state troops are mustering, but we have not seen any. Do you know of any enlistments?" he asked.

The old man squinted at Esker. "You intend to join up, do ye?" He repositioned himself to look Esker in the eye. "No. They's no troops here yet, but they are musterin' in Gainesville and Dallas." He looked around them to make sure they were not overheard. "Another buncha idjits if you ask me," he said.

"They's all over Gainesville, wavin' flags and marchin' up and down the street. All we are gonna get outta that bunch is over-run by the Comanche, and maybe the Kioway, too." He tilted his bottle up, and draining its contents, smacked his lips.

"You boys needn't worry. They will be comin' to find ya soon enough," he laughed. "They already got this Provost Marshal lookin' for layabouts. If you don't agree to join up, why they'll make ye, or hang ye, whichever suits your tastes. This Provost Marshal they got, his name is Gibbons. He has a prissy, trim little chin beard, and gold braid on his hat and his uniform, and he is so dainty he smells like candy," he slapped his knee and pointed at Esker. "If you aint a idjit, you would head west to the buffalo range. You join a frontier regiment and do work that is needful, instead of prancin' up and down the street a-waggin' a flag. You have to fight Comanches, though, and that is a fine vocation as long as you don't get caught. They'll gut ya, they will." He poked a thumb in the direction of Jackson. "I don't know if they will take that Injun, unless he is a tracker." He looked at Jackson and wrinkled his nose again. "What manner of Injun are you anyway?"

"Kickapoo," he replied. "I can track. I can read, too, can you?"

"Well, then, I will be a son-of-a-bitch." The old man rose unsteadily to his feet and staggered toward Jackson, brandishing his empty whiskey bottle. "I ain't gonna be spoke to in such a manner by a goddamned Injun." Jackson stood and swept the old man's feet from under him with the blade of his foot. The man was still cursing and throwing empty bottles at them when they mounted and rode west out of town.

CHAPTER 18

They rode until they crossed the Clear Fork of the Trinity. The water was slow and shallow and turbid, belying its name. They concealed their camp in a plum thicket by the river. Little green plums covered the bushes and they made Esker think of the good jelly his mother had made of them. He dragged firewood into camp and Jackson picketed the mounts. They cooked some salt pork and fried a little dough in the grease. They were silent through their meal until Esker wiped his hands on his shirt and asked,

"Well, has this trip satisfied your zeal for John Bunyan, Pilgrim?" Jackson, at first puzzled, broke into a broad grin.

"I should hope it has, Esker. At least we have had no monsters to fight."

"I suppose you should have said 'of late'." The thought of the vigilantes and his killing of Orvis Peck cast a shadow on his mood. "I hope we don't have too many monsters yet to bear."

By going due west from Fort Worth, they hoped to intersect and cross the Brazos River, the boundary between settled and wild countries. The travel, however, became more difficult. The land changed from rolling prairie dissected by little creeks to steep and angular buttes and little mesas. The ground was rocky and travel was hard on the mounts, who had become balky. On the second day, they entered a steep, wooded country with oaks and greenbrier thickets. The forest ran generally north and south. Jackson said he thought it was the western band of the Cross Timbers. Unlike its eastern cousin, which was park-like, this one looked impenetrable. They decided to abandon the thickets for the sake of their mounts and for themselves. Esker had already received bloody scratches from the abundant greenbrier and one of his shirtsleeves had been entirely ripped away by low hanging branches. Jackson, unscathed by comparison, knew when to duck. They paralleled the forest and traveled south to avoid further wear. After a day's travel, a distant cone-shaped mountain alternately appeared on the horizon, and then disappeared from view when they crossed creek bottoms and valleys, only to reappear when they regained the high ground. It was a curiosity, and it lay in the path of their travel.

"I have heard of it," said Esker. "I think they call it Comanche Peak, and the Brazos runs beside it."

CHAPTER 19

Fort Spunky lay at the foot of Comanche Peak. It had been a successful Torrey Brothers trading post for the neighboring peaceful tribes--Caddo, Waco, Tawakoni and others, before they had been forcibly moved to reservations in the late fifties. The settlement had never shined, but had lost any symptom of prosperity it may have formerly exhibited. A few years into its decline, someone named the place Fort Spunky because of the belligerence of the residents there, and the name had stuck.

When they rode into the settlement, relieved to have finally reached the Brazos, two men wrestled in a flooded ditch. One attempted to hold the other's head underwater, while calling him a "goddamned son of a bitch", but the other managed to flatten the first's nose with a rock. As the first lay face down in the water, the other attempted to compose himself by tucking his shirt tail into his breeches. He was covered with mud. On top of his head, he sported a clump of wet sod from which sprouted a tall weed. The effect was so comical as to make Esker and Jackson laugh until they could hardly keep their saddles.

The man observed their mirth and, not wanting to be the object of fun, adjusted his clothing again. He dragged his adversary from the ditch; rolled him onto his back; discovered the mud and weed on his head when he attempted to place his hat there; and then, bowing slightly to the boys, squished his way to the nearest saloon.

Rubbish covered the muddy streets of the settlement, and the air was redolent with piss. The rubbish irked Esker, not because of his high standards of hygiene, but because of its wastefulness. Much of it appeared to have some remaining use. He dismounted and picked up a badly chipped but serviceable chamber pot. He commented to Jackson that it must have been the last in town as the smell indicated all of its residents relieved themselves outdoors.

Their mounts had lost flesh on the long trip, and Jackson's mare needed shoeing. They decided to spend one or two days resting them. They also wanted to inquire about the duties and location of the frontier regiments, and their likelihood of encountering Comanche on their route west. They passed through town and made camp along the east bank of the river. A shallow ford lay nearby.

After grazing them for a day, they walked the mule and mare back to town and found a blacksmith. His shop was a lean-to which had been patched so many times and with such a variety of material, it looked to Esker like a patchwork quilt. The blacksmith was friendly, and he told them he could complete the job that morning. Esker counted the remaining coins he had stolen from Peck. The amount was sufficient, the blacksmith said, to shoe the horse and for them to get royally drunk while they waited at the Pigtown Saloon, which was across the street. A man lay on a board sidewalk at its front door. He hung his head over its edge and vomited enthusiastically.

"You fellers ain't preachers 'ere ya?" asked the blacksmith, who nodded disdainfully at the vomiter.

"No," replied Esker, but Brother Jackson here was an assistant to a Methodist minister."

The blacksmith sucked his teeth. "We need much reformin' here at Fort Spunky. Most of the men stay drunk all of the time. Nothin' gets done but drinkin' and arguin' and fightin' and pissin' on the buildin's," he said, disgusted. "We could use a preacher to show 'em the error of their ways and such." He turned to his work and they left in search of a place to replenish their supplies.

"Well, Brother Jackson, are you going to gather sheaves?" asked Esker as they walked away from the shop and the vomiting man. His eyes twinkled. "Why, you could gather a congregation here who would shout 'Hallelujah' to the rafters and pay you a tithe, and you could be invited to all the Sunday suppers with the pretty daughters to woo."

Jackson was a little embarrassed. "I don't believe any of that, Esker," he whispered. "It would not be honest." Esker was surprised.

"Are you not Christian, Andrew Jackson?"

"I learned scripture to please Pastor Simmons," he said. "I suppose it piqued my curiosity in a literary way."

"Are you not religious at all?" marveled Esker.

"I suppose my religion, such as it is, concerns faith in rain and sky and earth, which I have found usually dependable, and the possibility of there being good men which ain't. He was one, Simmons, though I don't see his religion making him so. He just was."

"Well, when I heard you read scripture, you sounded like a believer," Esker shook his head in astonishment. "You fooled me." He felt a little betrayed.

Jackson shrugged and smiled apologetically. "I am sorry, Esker. That was not my intention."

A clean-shaven man in a white shirt, possibly the cleanest shirt in town, stood under a clean, white canvas awning. Gathered around him were goods of various sorts. There were bags of meal and flour, dried beans, canned goods, and some hardware. All were new, and the meal and flour were without worms, though the sides of bacon, which hung from the awning, were fly-blown as usual. Esker had never seen store bacon which was not green. They bought flour, some salt pork, and the few other items their scarce resources would allow them. The clean merchant watched Jackson with unveiled suspicion.

"What kind of undertaking do you fellers aspire to?" he asked, after squirting a copious load of tobacco juice at a cat several yards beyond the awning while managing somehow to keep his white shirt unsullied. The cat, gravely offended, hissed and crawled under a stack of crates. Esker decided they were far enough west and beyond the vigilantes to reveal their intentions.

"We are seeking a frontier regiment sir, and might inquire of you as to where to find one," he said.

"We would also care to know the disposition of the Comanche on the road west," added Jackson.

The man cackled, "The disposition of the Comanche?" he mocked. "Their disposition?" he laughed. "They is mean as a snake! That is their disposition. But if you are inquiring as to whether you will lose your hair, I should answer yes, if you plan to travel more than three days west of here." He moved closer to them and pushed his face into theirs. "As to your other question, I assume you are avoiding the conscription," he sneered and spat another stream of tobacco juice away from his goods, but closer to the boys. Then he smirked. "We have had a number of young boys through here in the past few weeks. If you would prefer to be scalped instead of bein' peppered with grapeshot, I shall not stand in your way." He peered down the street, and spoke in hushed tones. "I will tell you this, and you do well to heed it. Get evidence of your affiliation one way or another. Marshal Law has been declared, and you need a pass to travel between counties. There is a Provost Marshal who comes to town once a month. Snatches boys and takes them off to serve the cause." He squinted at Jackson. "You a Mexican? Or some kinda Indian?"

"I am Kickapoo, sir'" said Jackson. "I do not know if my people have a treaty with either side, so conscription may not apply."

"Used to be a few Kickapoos lived with the Ioni here before Major Neighbours gathered them all up and pushed 'em in a herd to the reservation. We got along tolerable well with the whole bunch. Ruined business when they departed, it did. You would do well to get an affy davy from the magistrate here, committing you to a tenure with the frontier guard. It's not a military issue, as required and I can't guarantee that will keep that hard ass Marshal off you, but it may be the best you can do."

They found the Justice of the Peace in a shack next to the saloon. He was drunk, and had tobacco stains in his beard, but he was familiar with the need to provide bona fides to those men escaping the eastern part of the state. The judge told the boys that the frontier lay another few days ride to the west. He believed the closest regiments were forming in and around Hamerton County, which had recently suffered its share of Indian depredations.

"Well I suppose we should press on," said Esker. "Perhaps they will receive us with a parade."

CHAPTER 20

With their affidavits in their jackets, provisions replenished, and mounts rested, they were prepared to cross the Brazos River, the boundary between the tame place and the wild. The ford was shallow and easy, and the crossing took less than five minutes.

"I was expecting a little more pomp, given its mighty reputation," said Esker. Jackson smiled and pointed at debris hanging from limbs high above the channel.

"I suppose it depends on the day one crosses," he said. "This amount of pomp is sufficient for me."

They climbed a steep terrace and passed through alternately timbered and open country, where there were few occupied, but many abandoned cabins. After a day's travel there were no signs of settlement at all. Esker commented that the air felt different west of the Brazos.

"Well, it's wild here, Esker," replied Jackson. "It is just the way wild places feel."

"Well, the feeling makes me a bit skittish. I have to look over my shoulder," he replied.

"A good thing," observed Jackson. "Wild places are full of wild things, and sometimes wild people. It is good to keep an active frame of mind."

They had been on the trail for two days when a rise above a sizable creek, a Brazos tributary, gave them a view of green fields of corn and a few scattered, low domed grass and brush houses. Andrew Jackson gaped at Esker, hooted, and then kicked his horse into a gallop. He outdistanced Esker by half a mile, who followed him cautiously into the village where he was greeted by a pack of dogs. Most of the dogs wagged their tails and were friendly, but a mangy yellow dog with red eyes persisted in nipping at the mule's feet. The mule danced a few steps, and then deftly kicked the dog over one of the low grass houses, which amused some children who laughed from their doorway. Jackson had dismounted, and was talking to an Indian. The man was middle aged, and his black hair was cropped even with the line of his jaw. Except for his moccasins and a red blanket across his shoulder, he wore white men's clothes. Esker listened as Jackson spoke to the man in an incomprehensible language. He turned to Esker, smiling ecstatically and said,

"These folk are Kickapoo, and they have invited us to eat with them!"

There were three families living in the village, making up a population of eighteen, equally divided among men, women and children. They had rich fields and an abundance of food, which they were glad to share. Esker was reminded of a Christmas dinner, with everyone happy to see each other, and happy to feed strangers. It was an occasion.

By late afternoon, roasted ears of corn, squash and boiled venison were laid out in heaping bowls on the ground. The men sat in an inner circle, with women and children making two concentric rings around them. The man wearing the red blanket had been introduced as Joseph Blue Bill, the head man of the little group. Before they began eating, he crossed himself, and offered a prayer over the meal. The men ate their fill of the food, and then the bowls were taken by the women and then children. The food was abundant, and no one went hungry.

When the meal was finished, the men pulled clay pipes from beaded bags and smoked. Pipes were provided for Esker and Jackson, though neither cared for tobacco. They lit them and smacked their lips in appreciation, but let the pipes go out after a few puffs. Joseph Blue Bill stood and looked around the assembled group. He was preparing to make an after dinner speech. He directed his comments to Jackson, who interpreted for Esker.

"We Kickapoos have lived in Texas a long time. We liked our neighbors on the river, the Waco, Tawakoni and Tonkawa. Only the Comanche were our enemies, but they liked to eat our corn and steal our horses more than they liked killing us. Then the Texans came. They made a trading post near our villages, and that was good. We brought them skins and pelts and they gave us good things in return. They helped us keep the Comanche away. Our young men did not go crazy drinking the traders' whiskey like some of the others did. This was a good time. Then the Texans decided we should go live on another piece of land and they made us move, far away from the river where we were happy. The land given to us was not as good, and we could not leave to hunt. Then the Texans wanted that land, and they made us move into the Territory, and live next to the Comanche. This was not a good time. The Comanche raided, the soil was thin and would not grow crops, and we were crowded with people we did not know. This little group here," he pointed to those seated around them, and smiled at the children, "decided to come back to where they were happiest. As long as the Comanche leave us alone, and the Texans don't come to take our land, we will stay here, and be happy."

Being a guest, it was incumbent on Jackson to say a few words. He stood.

"I am Little Hand of the northern Kickapoo. My friend and I are full, because of your hospitality. Kickapoo are the most generous and brave of all people. We are going to the West to fight the Comanche." There were nods and grunts of approval.

A young warrior, who wore few white man's clothes, and his hair in long, wrapped braids acknowledged the gathering and spoke. "I think it is good for Little Hand to be here. He is of the People. He is polite and knows how to act, but he has brought a white man with him. This white man may tell other white men where we are, and the Texans may come looking for us. This is not good. That is what I have to say." He stalked off to a nearby brush arbor where he sat in the gloom, and glared out at Esker. Joseph Blue Bill beckoned to Esker and Jackson. They and the other men followed him to the brush arbor.

They squeezed in, a bit too tightly for Esker, but it seemed to suit the Indians who sat shoulder to shoulder in the hot little space. Joseph Blue Bill stirred some ashes in the center, and dropped sweet-smelling cedar on it. After a few minutes of silence had passed and the cedar smoke had damped the smell of sweating bodies, Joseph Blue Bill spoke.

"My nephew here is called Whirlwind. It was impolite for him to speak the way he did at our feast. However, what he has said spoke for many here, though they were too polite to have said it themselves. It is good that we can talk now, though. I think this young white man should speak now, and let us know his intentions."

Esker listened uncomprehending, and watched Jackson's face, which registered alarm. He told Esker that the Kickapoos were concerned that he would tell the Texans where they were, and that he would make trouble for them.

"It is very important that you explain that you too, are fleeing the Texans, and you will not make trouble for the Kickapoo. Make sure they understand this," whispered Jackson. Esker shifted so he could speak to the circle.

"I am Esker Doyle, and I lived in a cabin on the Sulphur River. There were men—Texans—who did not like my family because they did not want the Confederacy." Esker spoke slowly to allow for interpretation. Jackson stopped Esker as he described, in Kickapoo, the schism between the white men. Joseph Blue Bill told him they were aware of the secession. Esker continued.

"These Texans killed my family and burned my home. They killed Jackson's adopted grandfather. They tried to kill us, but we escaped. We killed their leader, but I fear they will continue to pursue us. These are the same men who would want trouble for the Kickapoo. Like you, we are against them, and like you, we do not want to be found by them."

Jackson explained that if the Confederates caught them, they would be pressed into the military or executed. "We cannot get into the Territory because of their militia and the Comanche. We can, however, serve on the frontier against the Comanche. We think this will satisfy the Confederates."

The men were momentarily silent, and then began to whisper to each other. After a few minutes, Whirlwind spoke.

"I have traveled north and have talked with our kin along the Konza River. It is a bad time for them. They followed the man Kenekuk, and became like the Americans, and wore his clothes, and farmed and lived in the square houses. Still, the Americans took their good land, and moved them to bad. They prayed to Jesus, but still the soldiers killed them for the thefts and killings done by others. Now, the Americans fight each other. The gray jackets want these Kickapoo to kill blue jackets. The blue jackets want these Kickapoo to kill gray jackets. Each tells them 'if you don't, we will kill you and take your land.' I thought it might be a good thing to kill this white man. Now, I have decided he has a good heart, and those who would do us harm wish him harm as well. I have decided to help him get to the Comanche country. I think I will go with them and kill some Comanche, too."

The meeting ended, and Jackson spread his blanket on the ground between the cornfield and the lodges. The wind rustled the corn stalks and they made music like water running over stones in a creek. Jackson yawned and lay on his bed. Esker was already asleep when Whirlwind approached. He sat next to Jackson.

"I am an impolite man," he said. "Sometimes I ask questions or say things when I should not," he smiled. "You speak Kickapoo, and you look like a Kickapoo, but when I think of you, I do not see one."

"I was raised by white missionaries," Jackson said. "At the Shawnee Mission in Kansas," he added apologetically.

"Are you obligated to the whites?" he smiled. "I think you have escaped them. That man," he motioned to Esker, "is in no way your equal. Does he have power over you?" he said, and moved closer to Jackson. "In this place, you don't have to be a white man anymore. Maybe you would want to stay here with us and be one of the People again. I have a cousin. She would make a good wife."

"I am honored that you would ask me," said Jackson. "I have thought some of the same thoughts as you, but I think I will finish what I came here to do. Maybe I will come back. Maybe eat some more of your good food," he grinned. "I would like that."

"Do not wait too long, or you might become white forever," said Whirlwind.

CHAPTER 21

The red sun rose through the low fog, which mixed with the smoke of the camp. Jackson had slept poorly, thinking about what Whirlwind had said to him. He had not considered "becoming white forever," but decided without some act of will he might succumb. He and Esker saddled and packed their mounts long before Whirlwind emerged from his lodge. He carried no kit other than his bow and a pistol tucked in his belt. His face was painted with black and red streaks, and his hair was greased and bristled with hawk feathers. He was dressed for war. His wife closely followed him, treading on his heels as she tied the feathers and skin of a red bird in his hair. She turned him around, looked him over carefully one last time, and then released him to go catch his horse.

The village was awake and busy by the time they left. Whirlwind knew of the settlements in Hamerton County, and would serve as their guide. They rode out of the green creek valley and onto a dry plain cut deeply by little canyons and arroyos. On the western horizon, a tall, steep bluff reflected the red of the rising sun. They had traveled more than five miles by late morning. The country became rocky and the soil was thin, and the tall prairie grasses were fewer. Prickly pear and yucca filled the gaps between clumps of grama and bluestem. As they neared the escarpment, Whirlwind pointed to a low place on its face and spoke to Jackson, who interpreted.

"He says that is the place we will climb the bluff, but we will first water the horses at a river near its base," he said.

It was early afternoon when they reached a fast moving, shallow river with a limestone bed. They allowed the horses and the mule to drink their fill. The day was hot, and the cool water had taken on sweetness from the limestone. The men drank greedily upstream from their mounts. Whirlwind was the first to notice a party of four riders descending the opposite bank, a half mile downstream. They apparently intended to water their horses as well. However, one of the men shouted, and the little group quickly crossed the river and rode toward them.

As they approached, Esker could discern their gray and butternut uniforms. The officer in their lead wore an elaborate pillbox of a hat, garnished with gold braid. It was the Provost Marshal, Gibbons. Despite his fancy dress, he was as dirty as his subordinates and was irritated at the indignity of being filthy. He looked no older than Esker nor Jackson.

"Good afternoon, gentlemen," he said in the high nasal voice of a cultivated planter. He looked down from his horse at the two Indians and the white man at his feet. "I am Provost Marshal Lieutenant Gibbons, serving under Brigadier General Hebert to apprehend those who would flee service in our cause and to enforce articles of the current Martial Law effective upon the ground on which you now stand." He pointed at Esker.

"How old are you?"

"Nineteen years, sir," Esker replied, without looking up.

"Why are you not, sir, in the service of your country? You are old enough. It is your duty, and it is the law. Further, these red friends of yours are not allowed in Texas. That one," he pointed at Whirlwind, who had hunkered down to examine an interesting rock, "appears to be attired for the commission of unspeakable depredations."

"These men are Cherokee, allied with the Confederacy, sir," lied Esker as he fished around in his coat pocket from which he pulled his affidavit. "These men are scouts for the Frontier Regiment. I have here bona fides from the Justice of the Peace at Fort Spunky," the soldiers snickered at the mention of the fort, "verifying that I am enlisting with a Frontier Regiment at Hamerton County." Gibbons reached down and pulled the paper from Esker's hand. He peered at it through a monocle.

"This document was not issued by myself or another qualified officer. It is worth nothing." He signaled to a soldier with some chevrons on his sleeve. "Sergeant McCourty, place these men under arrest."

Three Kickapoo warriors emerged from the brush. They pointed rifles at the soldiers. Simultaneously, Whirlwind grabbed the Lieutenant's reins, and pressed the barrel of his old pistol into Gibbons's side. The soldiers fumbled frantically at their sidearms, but Lieutenant Gibbons, his voice a panicked trill, screamed,

"Stand down!!! Stand down, Sergeant McCourty!! Control your men!!"

Sergeant McCourty shook his head in disgust, and repeated the order to the soldiers. Whirlwind pulled his pistol from Gibbons' side and stepped away from his horse. Gibbons adjusted his elaborate hat and said,

"These allied Cherokee need to know their place, and you sir, have committed a grievous crime. I shall see that you are hanged!" Whirlwind stepped forward and pressed the barrel into Gibbons' side again. He slowly pulled the hammer back, so that Gibbons could appreciate each click as it was cocked. Gibbons blanched and his neat little chin beard trembled a little.

"Very well," his voice cracked. "We shall permit you to pass. However, we shall meet again, and you, sir," he said, pointing a trembling finger at Esker, "will be left to imagine the consequences of your treason." The little troop turned their horses and rode downstream. Gibbons turned in his saddle, and shrieked,

"Until that day, sir!! Until that day!"

The Kickapoo laughed and shouted insults at the retreating troops. Whirlwind clasped each of the three warriors by the hand. When the riders were out of sight, Esker fell to his knees and vomited. Jackson stood with the group of men. Whirlwind spoke to him. When they had finished talking, Jackson walked over to Esker who was still heaving, and sat next to him, grinning.

"Their suspicion of you saved us, Esker," he laughed and gestured to the three warriors. "They were not sure you were a good man, so they followed us in the interest of protecting Whirlwind. If not for their queasiness about you, we would surely have been prisoners."

Esker wiped his mouth with the back of his hand. "I suppose we are safe for now, but I think we would be wise to leave as quickly as possible," he said hoarsely. "They may be preparing an ambush for us."

Jackson said, "The Kickapoo have agreed to accompany us over the escarpment. It will not be more than a day or two before we are in Hamerton County." He stood and looked down river. "I think we should enlist as quickly as possible. Though it might not satisfy that little rooster, it might make it more difficult to extract us."

There was a rough switchback up the escarpment. It was a dim trail between scattered boulders. Esker would not have known it was there, but it seemed familiar to the Kickapoo. Even Jackson, who had never traveled in this country, was able to follow it. They led their mounts up the last few hundred feet and rested at the rim. They looked back across the vastness a thousand feet below.

Whirlwind sat down next to Jackson. They gazed at the landscape before them in silence for some time. He said,

"When I was young, before the troubles began, my Uncle brought me here many times. Sometimes we saw buffalo turn the land black with their many bodies, but no more. Since we came back, I have seen no more buffalo than I can count on my hands. I think that I shall go back to the village. The Texans know we are here, and things could go bad for the People."

"The white man, Esker, told them you were Cherokee and allied to the Confederacy. They may not look for a few Kickapoo who just want to be happy in the river bottoms," said Jackson. Whirlwind did not register the comment, but said,

"There is much talk now about moving away from the Americans and the Texans. I do not think we can live as Kickapoo in the presence of so many white men. Our kin to the south have told us the Mexicans will give us much land, and will leave us alone. Our kin to the north are preparing to go. It will be a long journey getting there. In Mexico, we can be as numerous as we once were. We can live like the Kickapoo people again," he smiled at Jackson, "and not as imitations of white men." Jackson was stung by the comment and cast a glance at his white man's clothes. Whirlwind continued,

"I am going back. I think I will kill Comanches another time."

Whirlwind and the three warriors descended the trail and were almost out of sight when the sun slipped over the horizon. Esker and Jackson had been given roasting ears, and they cooked them in their husks. The day had blazed hot, but the night cooled enough that they kept the small fire going for warmth. They would make the settlements of Hamerton County the following day.

CHAPTER 22

The cool of the night dissipated quickly and by mid-morning heat waves shimmered off the limestone hills, and hot cicadas buzzed in the grass like rattlesnakes. Esker was glad they had filled their canteens at the river, but doubted the water would last long on so hot a day. The sweat stung his eyes, and deerflies bit them until they cleared the cedar brakes.

Now out of the cedar, they saw a broad, lush valley bordered by low mountains to the west. Whirlwind had said he believed the valley was the northern part of Hamerton County, but he said the Texans had not marked the boundaries in any particular way so he was not sure. They reached the valley in mid-afternoon. The grass was thick as dog's hair, and so high it swept the flanks of their mounts. Limestone knobs poked through the prairie at intervals, and they occasionally crested one to scout the surrounding country. Jackson spotted a small herd of antelope, who stared at them from almost a mile away, then disappeared like a cloud shadow. They emerged on another more distant knoll and resumed staring. Jackson touched the butt of his rifle when he saw them, then patted it and smiled sheepishly.

"I am hungry, Esker, but not that much of a marksman. It would be a shame to starve on the very eve of our arrival."

Esker agreed, and his nod was punctuated by a growl from his stomach loud enough to make his mule flinch. Esker spotted a commotion not far from the knoll where the antelope had fled. The grass riffled though there was no wind.

86

They rode forward to investigate. As they drew closer, they discovered the source. Three wolves were fighting over the carcass of an antelope fawn. The antelope herd was not far off, and they watched in apparent horror.

"Hurrah!!" shouted Esker, who kicked his mule and drew his pistol. He fired a few shots in the air, and the wolves fled.

When Jackson caught up, he asked, "Are you up to eating carrion, Esker?"

"Oh, no. This is a fresh kill. The blood on the ground is still wet, and there ain't a fly on him!"

The nearest source of wood for a cook fire was a creek bottom several miles away. By the time they were half-way, a swarm of flies found them and matched their pace, even though they maintained a trot. The little fawn was draped behind the horn of Esker's saddle, and the flies waited their turn at the carcass by resting on his nose, eyes and hat brim. He swatted furiously without effect.

"Dad-gum, Esker!" exclaimed Jackson. "It is a rank and dirty man who can lure flies away from a dead animal!" Esker gave him an evil look and continued his swatting.

"You needn't cuss me, Jackson."

They roasted the fawn in the shade of the creek bottom, and ate everything but the hair and hoofs. Jackson offered Esker an eye and half the brain, but he declined. The air was cooler by the creek, whose water flowed clear over gravel. By the time they each finished their portion of antelope, it was close to nightfall, so they picketed their mounts and lay down to sleep.

Just before sunrise, the smoke of a grassfire woke them. Esker, disoriented by sleep, ran to their cook fire and stomped it fiercely with his bare feet, but it was cold. The little gallery of trees along the creek held the smoke around them like wraiths caught in their branches. They gathered what little gear they had, mounted, then crested the nearest hill. On the far side of the creek, they saw a thin line of bright fire burning the prairie black as it crept through the dew-wetted grass. About a mile beyond, they saw a cabin blazing. Orange and yellow flames billowed from the windows, and black smoke rolled along the ground.

They descended the hill, crossed the creek and the thin line of flame. When they reached the cabin, they at first thought no one was home. Then Jackson found the first of four bodies. A child lay in the grass in its nightshirt, his head so brutalized it no longer looked like a head. The pitiful family was scattered across the dooryard. To Esker, they looked like bags of flour splashed with red paint: white bedclothes, white skin bled out, and blood soaking into the dry soil.

A shed was still intact. Jackson dismounted and searched it for a spade to dig graves. Esker sat on his horse, speechless, barely able to keep his stomach settled.

"Come, Esker. I suppose we can be of some service." He looked at the corpse nearest him and pointed. "Those are Comanche arrows." He shook his head and looked at Esker earnestly. "It seems we have come to the right place to fight Comanche."

CHAPTER 23

Two Bellies topped the ridge west of the burning cabin. He had reluctantly agreed to sponsor a few young warriors on their first raid. They were eager for war and glory. One of them wanted desperately to marry, and needed horses and scalps to win his bride. Two Bellies sympathized and, after much flattery and cajoling by the youngsters, he agreed. He liked to stay with his new wife, who was young and pretty. She smelled good. He would sit for an hour or more, while she brushed and braided his hair. He was no longer very young, and had come to enjoy his comforts. These Texans were easy to kill. The man ran out the cabin door and shouted at them once, then was killed by three arrows shot simultaneously from the over-eager warriors, who argued over rights to his scalp. The rest they brained with their clubs. Now they had three horses and a mule, a bolt of calico cloth, a few knives and three scalps. There was not much scalp left to take from one of the children. He would let the warriors keep the scalps, horses and mule, but he wanted to make a gift to his wife of the knives and cloth.

He paused on the ridge to admire the burning cabin, which was now totally engulfed. He saw Esker and Jackson digging with the spade. One of the warriors rode back to see what delayed him.

"I think we should go back and kill them," he said. "That is a good-looking horse, and we might need to eat that mule on the trip home."

"No. We have enough. Other Texans might see the smoke and come soon," said Two Bellies, which was true, though he mainly wanted to go home to his wife and her brush and her good smells.

He was puzzled. For many years, the blue coat soldiers had maintained forts along the edge of the Texan settlements. All through those years, his band, the Penateka, had been careful to thread their way between the forts without detection, raid houses and steal horses, and then thread their way back to safety. Then the blue coats abandoned the forts. At first he thought it was a trick, but soon grey-coated soldiers occupied some, but not all of the forts. One day, the grey coats disappeared. Raiding had become very easy. There were no soldiers, and most of the whites living west of the line of settlements had fled. Those who were left were easy to kill. Occasionally, his people came upon abandoned cabins or dugouts, and found goods left in them. Once he found a cask of black, sticky substance, so sweet it made his teeth hurt. His wife gave it to his mother-in-law, but she poured it on the ground after tasting it and scolded him for bringing home worthless stuff.

The raiding party entered the woody screen of the Cross Timbers, and rode north in dappled shade most of the way home into the Territory. While he rode, Two Bellies wondered at the peculiar state of things. His people had once numbered more than a thousand, and had lived many miles south, in the hill and limestone country of Texas. War with the Texans and the Texans' diseases and their goods, especially whiskey, had decimated the band physically and morally so that their numbers were few and they no longer resembled the people he had known as a young man. His little group numbered in the fifties, and each year, there were fewer young warriors coming to manhood. They died from the Texans' rifles and they died from their sicknesses. The women sometimes ate herbs to make their pregnancies stop, and the young men were not replaced. The Penateka had tried bravely to drive the Texans back down the Brazos and out of their hunting grounds. But more always came to replace them. There seemed to be a never-ending supply of them, no matter how many they killed. Now, for some reason, they abandoned the forts, and they abandoned their houses in the river valleys. Two Bellies wanted to find out why this had happened. In the meantime, the young men would want to raid as long and as frequently as they could.

They joined their band a few days later on the Washita River in the Territory. They crested a terrace above the river where Two Bellies beheld their camp in the setting sun. The lodges faced east, and the low angle of light penetrated the skin covers making them glow orange and white. Cook fires outside made good smells, and the women moved between lodge and hearth tending their chores. His heart swelled. The young warriors made the war cry, and charged into the village brandishing scalps and showing off their new horses. Two Bellies lingered behind. He smiled. No young man had been lost. They had trophies, and good reason to be proud. He looked south, back toward Texas. The next raid would be grander, he thought.

CHAPTER 24

Esker and Jackson finished burying the corpses near the cabin and said a few words sufficiently religious that they decided they had provided a proper Christian burial. They returned to the creek and followed it downstream, expecting to encounter the Leon River. They were told by Whirlwind that there were two settlements along the river, the larger being Hamerton, named for the county whose center it occupied. It began to rain, which added to the gloom of just having buried the little family. The creek passed through steep rock bluffs and the thunder crashed and echoed between them. Esker was apprehensive of being caught in a flash flood, and they gained high ground and hunkered under their mounts. After waiting out the worst of the downpour, they resumed their trek toward the river.

They were relieved to be nearing their destination, but had become apprehensive that a last-minute catastrophe might befall them, making the past months' efforts come to naught. The tension made them terse with each other. The creek finally joined a large, muddy river which roared past, pushing clots of foam and whirlpools big enough to swallow a boat, let alone swimming horses and riders.

"Well, I suppose this is the much ballyhooed Leon River. You think we will get across before Christmas?" mused Esker, who had cocked one leg over his saddle, and stared at the river, dejected. "Perhaps we could build a bridge."

"Do you suppose there is a ferry?" asked Jackson.

"Do you see a damned ferry?!" snapped Esker.

"No, Esker, I do not," Jackson calmly replied. "But it is probable that one exists along the river. I am sure this is not the first time it has run high. Some enterprising man has likely fixed one somewhere convenient to the settlements."

"Let's go find your dang ferry, then," said Esker, who found Jackson's elocution irritating.

They had followed the Leon downstream a half day when Jackson spotted some cabins on the opposite shore, on a bluff overlooking the river. A crude ferry was lashed to the opposite bank. Esker and Jackson hallooed for almost an hour. The rain had freshened and the brims of their hats dripped as they waited. A curtain of mist hung between them and the far shore. Scattered lamplight began to show through the windows of the few little houses, which looked like they had sprouted from the river bluff itself. Eventually, an old man carefully worked his way down the muddy slope. Twice he slipped and slid down the bluff on the seat of his britches. His mouth flapped, but they could not hear what he was saying. He untied the ferry, and as he pulled it closer, they began to hear his stream of profanity concerning their character, the nature of the river, as well as his bad luck.

"I should charge you both a goddamned five dollars for gettin' me out in this weather!" he shouted above the din of the river and rain. "What the hell are you doin' that is so fired important to inconvenience me so?"

They boarded the ferry and the man began to drag it to the other shore. Esker told him their intention to join a frontier regiment. The old man laughed at them.

"There ain't no damned frontier regiment! Not any short of the Red River or the Rio Bravo, anyway. You missed it by a month!" He spewed tobacco juice into the river then looked at them through a squinty eye. "Jeff Davis just called all those local boys to the front back east. I reckon if you ride as fast as you can, you might catch 'em in Arkansas!" The news startled them.

"Shit," hissed Esker. "You mean we came all this way for nothin'?" He pulled his affidavit from his pocket, wadded it up, and threw it in the river. Jackson was silent, and calmly watched the brown water rush past. He turned to the old man.

"What settlement is this?" he shouted.

"Evermore!!" shouted the old man.

They spent a wet and miserable night with a milch cow in the ferryman's cramped little barn. The morning was somber and overcast, but the rain had diminished to a steady drizzle. The ferryman did not offer food or coffee, and they did not risk his ire in asking. He had charged them, in addition to the ferry fee, fifty cents each for livery and the luxury of sleeping with his cow. He softened a little.

"Well... I heared that a man can join up with a frontier defense company, if you are that eager to fight Comanches," he said. "You must be from one of the counties in the district, I suppose." He squinted at them. "You ain't fleein' the conscription ere ya?"

Esker sneered, "What kind of fool would do that?"

They were cheered a little that they still might find a military occupation of sorts, and rode out of the little town to find the military road to Hamerton, which the ferryman said ran from old Fort Gates north and west.

After a few miles, they stopped to eat the few remaining scraps of salt pork and share a can of tomatoes which made up the last of their larder. Both of them had become gaunt. Jackson's hair had grown past his shoulders. Esker had sprouted a scant yellow beard, which made his face look dirty instead of hairy. Jackson looked at Esker, and laughed.

"Esker Doyle, you are one ugly white man. I can smell you ten feet away, too! You out-smell the horses!"

Esker grinned and threw a wood chip at Jackson. "Physician, heal thy self!! You look more Indian than old Whirlwind, and I can smell you, too!! Besides, Indians smell worse than white men. Everybody knows that."

Jackson stared balefully at Esker. Then he broke into a grin and laughed, which started Esker. They laughed so hard and loud, their mounts grew nervous.

After their assessment of each other, they agreed it would be a good idea to clean up at the next stream which was not too deep for bathing. They wanted any first impressions at Hamerton to be good ones. After swimming their horses across two muddy clay-bottomed creeks, they found a shallow, clear stream with a limestone bed. Live oaks made a canopy over the stream, which was not more than six feet across. They stripped and washed their clothes and bathed in the cold water. Esker pulled on his oiled canvas and shivered while he dragged a dull knife across his bristled cheeks. Jackson sat, naked and shivering, and watched Esker attempt to shave. He fingered his long hair thoughtfully.

"I think I am going to keep my hair long. Maybe braid it. I think it might be good to go back to being Kickapoo again." He was thinking about Whirlwind's comment concerning "imitation white men". He felt indicted by it.

"If that suits you, Jackson," said Esker. "Besides, if we fall in with the rangers, they might believe you can track. Just keep your glasses in your pocket."

"I only need them to read, Esker. I suppose I may slip them on should I need to closely examine a track," Jackson replied.

"Well, I have never seen an Indian who wore glasses," said Esker. "The rangers might not believe you … but then I don't suppose I have seen that many Indians to judge by."

CHAPTER 25

A little creek ran adjacent to the town, but because of the recent deluge, it was no longer little. It ran wide, muddy and flat, and swept through a stand of tall pecan trees which held debris from the flood, including several old tents. Their recent inhabitants stood on the far side of the creek and looked at them forlornly. Esker and Jackson checked their mounts and assessed the water. Beyond the creek and scattered across the hillsides stood a few more dirty white tents. The town was otherwise a mud puddle with a sprinkling of clapboard and stone buildings. Those closest to the creek were wet up to the window sills. Every chimney in town was billowing smoke, which rolled along the ground and between buildings like a thick fog. Their tenants were trying to dry their rooms and belongings.

"Well, it don't look too deep, but it is running awful fast," Esker yelled over the roar of the flood. On the west side of the creek, a man hollered to them, his hands cupped around his mouth.

Jackson said, "He appears to be telling us something about the crossing. I believe he is directing us to a better ford." They followed the creek and eventually found a meander where rocks and debris forced the creek to narrow. They swam their mounts across and climbed the opposing bank after floating a few yards downstream. They emerged on a street flanked by a row of mostly unpainted clapboard buildings. They were all saloons. Several had muddy water flowing through their front doors. The flood, though, had little impact on the saloon business, as attested to by the number of horses tied before them.

"We could inquire in there about the frontier service," said Jackson, pointing at the door of the nearest saloon.

"Suits me," replied Esker. He dismounted, and as an afterthought turned his dripping pockets inside out. "I guess we ain't heeled to buy," he grinned.

The saloon was so dark, Esker tripped over a spittoon, spilling its contents. The mess made little difference, as most of the patrons eschewed such conveniences, preferring to spit on the floor. The clatter, however, drew the attention of four or five men at the bar and about as many at the tables scattered around the room. Conversation ceased and they all stared at Esker and Jackson.

"I will not suffer goddamned Indians stinking up my establishment!!" brayed the bartender, who pulled a long chunk of stove wood from behind the bar.

"My mistake, gentlemen," replied Jackson, who tipped his hat and dashed through the door and into the street.

"I am Esker Doyle, and I ain't a Indian," hollered Esker. He grinned around at the customers, and then the bartender. They did not grin back. "I came in to inquire about opportunities to join the frontier service. That Indian is my tracker, and I can ride and shoot. Sometimes at the same time," he added nervously. The latter comment made the bartender chuckle.

"Well, in that case, I suppose you should talk to Captain Price. He has a mercantile two streets over, by the creek. Just don't bring me any more Indians, even if they are scouts."

Captain Price was in his store, salvaging what few goods he had. His flour and sugar would have been considered ruined and unsellable before the war, but he spread them on a wagon sheet to dry.

"This dang frackus has nearly ruined me," he said mildly. "Ain't got much to sell, but if you and your partner want to sit on the floor and suckle a corner of a wagon sheet for nourishment, it will cost you two cents each."

"We are in no position to buy, Captain," said Esker. "I am Esker Doyle, and this is Andrew Jackson. We are seeking to enlist in the frontier defense." Captain Price stroked his mass of black chin whiskers, and scrutinized them.

"If you are from this county, I have not encountered either of you. Where is it you reside?" asked Price, who looked at them dubiously.

Esker paused. He knew the service was limited to the residents of those counties along the frontier. He guessed. "Why Coryell, Captain."

"I know most of the folks in that county," said Price. "I don't know you."

"We were way down on the Leon, Jackson and me. Our folks were in the woods and up in the cedars most of the time. I am not surprised that you did not know them. We intend to reside in this county as of today."

Price's shoulders sagged a little. "You are not the first I have met whose claims to residency are weak," he scowled. "In addition to keeping the Comanche problem to a simmer, I have the duty to round up deserters and shirkers to present to the Provost Marshal." He sullenly turned to his work, hanging the few remaining waterlogged sides of green bacon near the window. The flies swarmed at them with such gusto, they must have been waiting nearby for the table to be set.

Jackson spoke, "Captain Price, on our ride in from the northeast, we encountered a farm which had been raided by the Comanche. A family was killed, including two children. We buried them before we moved on."

"Oh, hell. Where was it?" demanded Price. An abrupt change passed over his face. His eyes pierced Jackson through his mass of black eyebrows and whiskers. "How long?!" he roared.

Jackson took a step back. "It was almost twenty miles northeast of Evermore. About five miles west of the escarpment in a broad valley," he said. Given his tone, Jackson thought Captain Price might consider him a suspect. "The blood was fresh and the cabin was still afire. That was two days ago."

Price sighed, and sat down on a hogshead of rusty nails. "That would be the Carney family," he said. "I told them to move into the settlements, but Mr. Carney was one to heed no advice but his own." He momentarily hid his face in his hands and rubbed his eyes. He squinted at Jackson. "What kind of Indian are you?" he asked.

"I am Kickapoo, Captain Price," replied Jackson, who stepped forward. "I can track. I read and write well, too."

"Well, I suppose we should go hunt up the squad and see what can be done," said Price wearily.

CHAPTER 26

They crossed the Leon north of the settlement with some trouble. The water was high and swift, but the ford was shallow enough for them to dismount and swim their horses. Two of the rangers were swept some yards downstream, but were able to make the other side and climb the steep bank. The others stood above them watching, chunking clods, making cat-calls and laughing. They were covered in yellow mud- even their beards were caked.

"It will all be under road dust in a day or two, I guess," said Captain Price, who was as muddy as the rest. There were fifteen in all, including Jackson and Esker. Other than the uniform covering of mud, there was nothing otherwise resembling a uniform among them. Most of them wore old and patched homespun clothes. Their hats were a mangy array of floppy wool felts and broad brimmed Mexican sombreros. Each man carried a revolver and long knife in his wide belt. Most carried shotguns across the pommel of their saddles.

Jackson was placed at the head of the column as scout, though he did not know the way. The rangers did. He guessed correctly that it was a test to determine his worth as a scout. He led the group northeast, and after a half day, he recognized the hills which bordered the western edge of the valley. Not long before sunset, the blackened skeleton of the little cabin came into view. The location of the graves was obvious. One containing the youngest child had been molested by varmints, and the little boy was scattered about.

Price ordered his men to collect and reinter him. He turned to Esker. "You did not see to it that he was buried deep enough." Esker explained that the ground was stony and shallow. Unlike the soil along the Sulphur River, they had hit rock within a few inches. "Next time, put more rocks on the grave, to keep the coyotes at bay," replied Price.

The stench riled Esker's stomach so that, at first, he was unable to answer. A weak "Yassir," was all he could manage.

Esker and the rangers tended to the burial. Jackson and Captain Price scouted the ground.

"The rain has scoured all but the deepest horse tracks," said Jackson, "but I conjecture there were four Comanche. There are four shod horses, too. One might be a mule. He seems a bit more flat-footed than the others," said Jackson. Captain Price stroked his beard, nodded approvingly.

They followed the trail to the ridge where Two Bellies entered the post oak woods. "Do you think they took a captive?" Captain Price pointed to a scrap of cloth clinging to a greenbrier thicket. Jackson dismounted and pulled the shred from the thorns.

"This cloth is new and mighty stiff from sizing," he said. "Too stiff to have been worn much. Maybe they stole a bolt of raw fabric." Captain Price smiled.

"I reckon the Comanche are already back in the Territory by now, but I intend to follow their trail far enough to determine they had no captives. I think all the Carneys are accounted for, but they may have had guests, or the miscreants may have raided elsewhere."

The company was reassembled, and they resumed their march north through the Cross Timbers. The rangers stopped and made camp long before Two Bellies' raiding party had even stopped for water. They built small cook fires and dragged up water in their cups and hats from a muddy little creek below the ridge. After they had had their bite of parched corn and a little jerked meat, their energy revived and a fair amount of joshing and squirming ensued.

A corporal with a crooked nose and bad breath named Woodrow whispered confidentially to Esker. "The goddamn Comanche know the land and the water, and have better mounts than we do," he caught a tobacco juice dribble before it landed on his shirt. "I have been rangin' with this bunch for all of eight months, and we done no more than to catch a glimpse of the rumps of their horses." He snickered, "Ain't that so, Mosey?"

Mosey was one of two second sergeants in the company. He was older and slower than the others. He was grizzled and worn. It seemed to Esker, that all of the rangers were non-commissioned officers or higher. All, that is, except he and Jackson. Mosey was slow to answer. He rubbed his hands across his stubbled face, and finally observed, slowly.

"Them Comanche are fast," he paused for another face rub, "They ride fast, they don't stop to eat, or even shit, in so much as I can surmise." He looked at Woodrow and Esker directly. "If'n we don't give up our sleep and our mess and find better mounts we won't ever engage them in battle." He paused to think. "Unless we just happen to fall over them ridin' around in the dark some night." He pictured that in his mind and

104

sucked his teeth. "I reckon that would frighten the wits out of me."

Eventually, Jackson and Esker rolled into their blankets to sleep. Esker wondered, "How did you learn to track? You were what...ten when you went to the mission?"

Jackson thought before answering. "I had two uncles who taught me. I would have learned more, though." They were quiet for a while. Just before Esker drifted off to sleep, Jackson whispered, "Where white men only look at things, Indians seem to see them, I think. I don't know why, but it appears to be true."

After another day of following the trail through the oaks and thickets, Price was satisfied that no captives had been taken on the raid, and further pursuit was a waste of time. The squad returned to the settlement, and took up the tedium of shoeing horses, repairing tack and cleaning the hastily slapped together barracks on the edge of town. The Price Company of the 2nd District Frontier Organization was divided into three squads of a dozen or so men, each serving monthly a ten-day obligation. Captain Price told Esker and Jackson he would enlist them on the honor of their oath of residency. Further, he had been sufficiently impressed with Jackson's tracking skills that he asked him to work through the duration.

"We sometimes use hounds for tracking," he explained, "But you are moderately easier to talk to." He offered him permanent lodging in the barracks and five Confederate dollars a month. Esker was dismayed. No one had offered him wages, and he rankled. He finally brought his discontent to his bunkies, who laughed in his face and slapped him on the back.

"Hell, boy," laughed Corporal Woodrow, "We are all supposed to be paid two dollars a month, but the state government ain't got a pot to piss in. They don't even pay for mounts or ammunition, anyway." The little crowd walked away, shaking their heads and hooting. Mosey sat in the shade of the barracks, taking in their snickering at Esker's expense. He beckoned him over.

"Boy, we all have to shift for ourselves the best we can. You need to find an occupation to carry you through the times you ain't rangerin'."

"But what is there to do for money?" Esker said. "Other than saloon work or livery, I ain't noticed much opportunity." Mosey smiled and picked at his broken fingernails.

"Well...most of us are hand-to-mouth, I reckon. We take any work we can find. Even the Captain fairs poorly. The fellers and I can ask about, but we will be hard pressed to turn down any opportunity ourselves. Money don't count for much anyway. Most folks barter. Trade a chicken for a sack of corn meal, or such." Esker nodded and walked off to the barracks. Jackson met him at the door.

"You appear out of sorts, Esker. Are you peaked?"

"Well, you might feel peaked too, if you were up and left by your friend," he said. He busied himself with adjusting the blanket on his cot.

"I judge this is about my promotion," he said. "It makes no difference, Esker. Besides, I will be happy to help you out until you get situated. Captain Price agreed for you to stay in the barracks until you find gainful employment. You can earn your keep cleaning and doing repairs."

"Why is it that you, an Injun, is the only one of us to get pay?" he sneered. His face was flushed.

"Because I will be on duty thirty days a month, Esker. And who do you think will rent a room to an Injun," he said, imitating Esker's tone. "Or hire one? But you suit yourself." Jackson turned and walked out the barracks door and into the bright light beyond.

CHAPTER 27

It was early fall. The low mountains south of Hamerton had been on fire intermittently for the past month. Mrs. Eudora Mabel Carson looked south, and admired the yellow haze, which softened the sunlight, and made the scenery shimmer gold. She had been told the Indians burned every fall to open up grazing for the buffalo, but she told her husband they did it to amuse her. She had a fine dog-run on a little hill almost a mile south of town near the road which connected it to Langford's Cove. She was a fastidious woman of thirty-five, whose luxurious childhood in South Carolina had given her expectations never met on the raw edge of the frontier. She had hardened over the years, and had become more like the land- dry and stony. She had roses and blooming shrubs shipped from New Orleans at great expense to soften the aspect of her rough but respectable home. Her husband, Albert Sydney, was a lawyer, but his fervor for the cause had compelled him to abandon her to enlist as a junior officer on the malarial coast at Galveston. They had no children, and few dogs. Albert Sydney wrote to her regularly. There had been no combat and only boredom and sickness since his arrival. In the year since his departure, he had been bed-ridden with typhus for half of it. His letters insisted that Eudora move to town. He fretted that some Comanche might kill her or worse.

"He should have thought of that before he ran off to the war," she thought. She had no intention of moving. She was comfortable alone in her cabin, and the people in the town were rough and dirty.

She wrote, "If I had a nigra or two, they would be of help. Alas, there are none to be found in the county." Instead, she wrote that she would hire a "reputable" man who could live in the smoke house. He would assist her with chores and be of some use should the Comanche bother her. She imagined her husband's jealousy at the idea, and it amused her. "Serves him right," she thought.

She worked in her garden and canned produce all summer. With the annual purchase of a hog, she was able to make do through the winter. Eudora was turning a bed for turnips. She liked to sink the fork into the soil she had made; to feel its firmness and depth. There were many chores which required her energy but they were ephemeral, would be needful of doing again and again. But her vegetable garden was a measure of who she was. It compensated for the lack; for the absence of company, the sere landscape; the limitations of frontier life. Her hilltop was a skinny place, with little soil and much rock. She hauled manure and rotten hay from the barn and had over the years built her garden into something which could not help but grow food.

The sun beat down through the smoky haze, and she stood to stretch her back and wipe the sweat from her eyes. She caught sight of a distant rider, who crested a hill and galloped north on the Cove road. His old mule looked like she was close to spent. She could see arrows embedded in the man's back. They flopped with the rhythm of the uneven gait of the mule. A band of Indians rode over the brow of a little hill south of her vantage point. They were mounted on small ponies which were neither fatigued nor slowing. They whooped and shot rifles and arrows at the man, who abandoned his mule in a little creek bottom just below her cabin. He knelt and fired his pistol at them. The mule, seeing Eudora's house and barn nearby, limped to her gate and waited. The Indians drew close, but were thwarted by the steady fire of the wounded man. One Indian shouted and fell from his pony. The others soon gathered him and fled. She rushed down the hill to aid the man, who sat with his legs splayed in front of him. The arrows bristled from his back like porcupine quills.

"I feel like lying down, but those danged arrows are in the way," he said. "They are a damnable nuisance."

He passed out and sagged forward, still sitting. She rolled him on his side, and examined his wounds. One of the arrows fell out when she moved him. Another was not too deep, but a third was imbedded deeply between his ribs. Captain Price and several rangers arrived shortly after. An Indian ran to the injured man's side.

He knelt and whispered urgently, "Esker!! Esker!! Can you hear me??"

The men made a litter, and moved him to Eudora Carson's dog-run. Her bedroom and a small sitting room made up one cabin. A dining room and a larger sitting area comprised the other. They were connected by a porch and breezeway. The men placed Esker in the dining room on a thick pallet of quilts she had laid for him.

"We need to send a man down to get the doctor," said Mrs. Carson to Captain Price, who stood at the doorway, watching.

"No need, Eudora, our scout left to fetch him some minutes ago."

The doctor, a garrulous, clean shaven man of seventy, examined Esker. He easily removed the shallowly seated arrow, and then turned his attention to the deeper, talking the while about all topics other than the one at hand. Captain Price cleared his throat.

"So, what is his prognosis, Doctor Fuhlendorf?"

The Doctor did not seem to hear him, but after fiddling with the last arrow and finishing his diatribe against the worthlessness of Confederate scrip, he stood and faced him.

"That last arrow is a bad one," he said, wiping blood from his hands on a rag. "It appears to be lodged next to his spine. I can't yank it out for fear of killing him, or at least paralyzing him." He knelt down next to Esker and gently moved the arrow shaft. "I can remove the shaft, but the point will have to stay. If the wound don't suppurate, it will encyst and he should live. If it putrefies, he shall die."

The squad loafed about the porch. Some peeked in the door from the breezeway. Sergeant Mosey shook his head sadly.

"Danged if he didn't last only a few months, and he's the first one we lost. Ain't none of us had more than a saddle sore until now."

"He isn't dead, yet," said Jackson, resentfully. "Esker may be back with us in a few weeks," he said. "He had just gone to the Cove to look for some goddamned work," he said mostly to himself. "I doubt that he found it."

The sound of hounds baying erupted from the creek bottom. Captain Price stepped out of the cabin. "It's time to mount up, fellers. The hounds have found the trail of the Indians." The troop mounted and straggled into the creek bottom. The tangle of men, horses and hounds eventually moved slowly south, up the rise and over its crest. The hounds led south; then turned northwest. The sun was low on the horizon before the hounds began to slow.

CHAPTER 28

Two Bellies lay on his back by a little creek between two limestone knobs. The bullet had grazed his temple, knocking him unconscious, but leaving him with no more than a bad headache and double vision. He saw two of everything, but the images were beginning to coalesce. The stars had come out. The day had not gone well, he thought, but the night was cool and pretty. They had taken no horses nor captives or scalps, and chasing the Texan had just been sport, and a mistake. Their paths had just intersected, and chasing him was too much temptation. The raiding party had stopped long enough to let their horses water and to let Two Bellies regain his equilibrium. A warrior named Hair Rope sat down next to him, and idly drew figures in the sand with a mesquite thorn.

"You have pretty good magic," he said. "I saw that the Texan would kill you, but your medicine made the bullet turn away." He smiled at Two Bellies and grasped his arm. "I think that is a good sign. I think we need to go take trophies and horses."

Two Bellies chuckled. Hair Rope rose and led his horse to him. He helped him mount. Two Bellies shook his head to clear it.

"The Texans are following us," he said. "I think I will go around these hills to the south. We might catch those rangers from behind." Hair Rope nodded in agreement.

"I think we will come with you."

The rangers followed the hounds north and west into hilly country above the Lampasas River. Little creeks passed between the hills, and it was hard to keep the hounds from lingering at the water. They had traveled over thirty miles and were footsore. A man named Packard and his son Bill were dog men. They both smelled like their hounds and Jackson thought they had an odd manner about them. The men dismounted and inspected their dogs' feet which they found skinned and bloody, and determined they were unfit for further travel.

"Jackson!" Captain Price craned his neck to find him in the dark. Jackson rode up. "I need you to keep on the Indians' trail. Scout up their track; then give us a signal. We will ride up to meet you."

The starlight was bright enough to see tracks, but the ground on which they had stopped was flinty. He rode out from the squad a hundred yards and swept a line perpendicular to what he suspected was the Comanches' direction of travel. He repeated this out to almost a third of a mile. At a little arroyo, he found where they had crossed; their unshod horse tracks clear in the loamy earth. The rangers mounted and followed.

Dawn broke. The sun shone red between the horizon and a heavy cloud deck which had moved in overnight. Jackson could easily follow the horse tracks now, but the trail had changed; had become confused. There were moccasin prints in addition to those of the horses. The Indians had stopped at a little creek bed. Jackson had dismounted and pulled his spectacles from his pocket when the first shot rang out from the rear of their column. The Indians charged them from behind and rode into the troop, using clubs and lances to devastating effect. Four rangers had fallen, and the troop was in such disarray that they were unable to turn their horses in time to counter the charge.

"Dismount and mass in the gully!!!" bellowed Captain Price, who emptied his pistol into the writhing cloud of dust.

The rangers who were not engaged in hand-to-hand fights dismounted and let their horses flee. Once they made the protection of the creek bank, they were able to use their shotguns and few rifles. Two Bellies signaled his warriors to retreat out of range. Price's squad had lost several men and now only ten clung to the edge of the creek bed. Jackson sat with his back against the creek bank, his rifle across his lap. After the noise and chaos of the fight, Jackson's ears rang in the deafening silence.

Sergeant Mosey said to Woodrow, "I knew we would end up stumblin' over them in the dark. Didn't I say so?"

Woodrow replied, "I think they stumbled over us. Besides, the sun is up. How many you think there are?"

"Maybe twenty. I think we killed two or three, though." Mosey peered over the bank to make a count. "Three," he said. "They got four of us. They didn't have time to take scalps, though."

Jackson peered over the creek bank. The Comanche were lined up as though they were on parade. They wanted to be seen and admired and feared. They were. Half of them were mounted on scrawny, short legged mustangs. The others were mounted on long legged grade horses stolen from little farms and ranches unfortunate enough to have been targets. All of the horses had notched ears. Most of the warriors carried long lances, festooned with scalps and ribbons. Several wore buffalo horn hats. They were otherwise naked except for leggings and loincloths. The dim sun glinted off their lances and their skin. They were an impressive sight.

A ranger named Albert Ross leapt to his feet and swatted at an arrow in his back as though a hornet had gotten in his shirt. Another hit him in his chest as he hopped around. He fell on his side.

"They're comin' up the creek boys!!" shouted Mosey.

Three Comanche hid themselves in the woody scrim upstream and loosed arrows into the knot of crouching rangers. In return, the rangers massed fire at the woods. Leaves rained down from the trees, but the Indians escaped.

On the signal of the firing of the rangers' shotguns and rifles, the Comanche whooped and charged the creek. The rangers had expended their charges in an instant and did not have time to reload. Those with pistols fired into the oncoming mass, and others pulled long knives in preparation for close combat. The charging Comanche closed the distance in seconds. They ran their horses through the shallow creek bed, and trampled one of the rangers to death. They made the far side of the creek, turned, and loosed a hail of arrows from horseback.

Captain Price yelled, "Charge the sons-of-bitches!!"

The half dozen still-able men poured out of the gulley, and ran into the mass of mounted Comanche. The rangers' pistols were deadly at close range, and several Indians were quickly unhorsed and on the ground, dead. Two Bellies signaled the party to retreat. They ran their horses into the chaparral on a nearby mountain. They had lost six warriors; too many to consider this a successful raid. There had been no opportunity to take scalps from their kills, and they had left all but two of their dead on the field. Two Bellies watched his warriors assemble and said,

"We will bury those men in the rocks, here. We will wait here until the Texans leave and get the others still on the ground."

Hair Rope was agitated. "The horses of the rangers are nearby. We should get them before they do. I did not come on this raid with you to go home with empty hands." The other warriors murmured. Two Bellies turned to them with the expression of a rattlesnake about to strike. They were silenced.

"You chose to come on this raid with me. We have lost too many warriors. I think we should go. However, you are all free men. If you want to chase the rangers' horses, you can chase horses." He sat on a rock and looked at them stubbornly. "I am going to bury my dead. You can bury yours."

Hair Rope mounted his horse and rode back into the valley to gather the horses. The sky was lowering and thunder muttered in the distance. The remaining warriors mounted and followed him, leaving Two Bellies sitting on his rock.

CHAPTER 29

"Do you think they are comin' back for another fight, Captain?" asked Corporal Woodrow. It had been over an hour since the Indians had disappeared near the little mountain.

"I suppose they went to gather our horses for us," he sighed without looking at him. "It's going to be a long walk home." It concerned him that the Comanche dead were still on the ground. It was unusual for them to leave their battle-killed behind. They would be back.

"Boys, we are going to start the long walk south," he said. "Let's bury our dead as best we can, and leave the field so the Comanche can do the same."

Albert Ross and the others were placed in shallow graves. Rocks were mounded over them. When they finished, Sergeant Mosey said,

"Shouldn't we say a kind word before we go?"

Captain Price motioned for the men to join him. He took off his hat. "Lord, these boys have done the best they could. Their parting is going to leave much sorrow at their homes. We will miss them too. We pray that you will be with them all." He put his hat on and said, "And us, too. Let's go. It looks like a storm is comin'."

The men gathered arms and ammunition from the dead to keep them from falling into the hands of the Indians. They were heavily burdened and their walk was slow. They crested a little mountain and scouted the terrain. They had not been followed, but could see the Indians, several miles distant, driving their horses north. Jackson admired the thunderhead. It took up much of the horizon in the northwest. The air below it was dark as midnight, and there were intermittent flashes of lightning beneath. His grandmother believed that the thunder beings talked to people, and though they were sometimes dangerous, might sometimes be helpful. He thought sometimes that they noticed him when they rolled slowly across the prairie. He smiled at them. He didn't know if they smiled back.

"It looks like a blue norther, for sure," groaned Corporal Woodrow. "If the Indians don't come back to finish us off, the cold might do as well." Captain Price ordered them to seek a sheltered place, where they could put some rock between themselves and the wind. No one disagreed.

They followed a narrow valley up to its top between two bluffs where it formed a steep canyon. The walls were shear rock, and a little grotto had formed at its head. They collected firewood from the abundant cedar and scrub oak growing above it. Shortly after they had built a good fire, the wind began blowing rain and sleet. The men had left town quickly in warm sunny weather, and few had packed slickers or coats. Those who had brought coats rested snugly against the canyon wall and grinned at the less fortunate. Once the thunderstorm passed, it began to snow. The men, cold and hungry, fell asleep as close to the fire as they dared.

Looks Behind Him and Elk Boy abandoned the horse herd and doubled back to take the scalps of the Texans they believed they had killed. The snow came down in big wet clots, and they shivered as they crossed the ridge back into the little valley.

"I hope those scalps are big and hairy enough to wear," Elk Boy said through chattering teeth.

Looks Behind Him just grunted and shivered. They had blankets, but like the rangers, were poorly dressed for the weather. They were the youngest warriors in the party, and had never taken scalps. They gave up their share of the horses to turn back. They pulled the rocks from the graves, and argued over which one had killed which ranger. Finally, they scalped and mutilated all the stiff corpses and left them on the ground for the buzzards and coyotes to fight over.

CHAPTER 30

It was almost a week before the squad walked into town. Their tardiness in returning had caused much anxiety among the families of those rangers who had them, and a great deal of speculation among the others. A few wives, mothers and sisters watched them straggle in, looking for husbands, sons and brothers. Of the six killed, three had relatives in town. Jackson watched Captain Price talk to the widows and the bereaved; watched him catch a woman as she sank to her knees, wailing. The piteous crying was too much for most of the squad, who entered the barracks and fell on their cots, exhausted. Sergeant Mosey and Jackson were the only ones still standing. They lingered by the barracks door.

"I'll swear," said Mosey, leaning against the door frame and rubbing his face. "Well, I'll swear," he said again. He was not able to attest to what he was about to swear to. He was speechless.

"I am going to see about Esker," said Jackson to Mosey. "I expect your rotation is up in the morning, so I will see you at the first of next month."

He walked up the Cove road toward Eudora Carson's house. The snow had melted and the road was muddy. He missed his horse, and did not care for being afoot. The sun was bright, but the wind was blowing cold and damp from the south. Jackson had lost his coat which was tied to his saddle, and wondered where he might find another of each. Smoke was rising from the chimney of the Carson cabin. He smelled coffee as he approached.

Eudora saw Jackson as he approached the house. His braids now hung almost to his waist, and he was armed and dirty. She cautiously opened the door a crack. Jackson stood at the bottom of the steps and said in a loud voice,

"I am Captain Price's scout and a friend to Esker Doyle. I have come to see about him."

"I remember you from the day they brought him in," she said, opening the door a little wider. "I guess you can come in." Jackson entered the room, and saw Esker, asleep on the pallet on the floor. His face was pale and bright with sweat.

"How is he?" asked Jackson. Eudora directed Jackson to sit on a little stool in the corner. The fireplace crackled and the room was warm, making his fatigue harder to battle.

"Well, he is alive," said Eudora who sat down on a little settee by the fire. "He had a terrible fever, which broke last night. Doctor Fuhlendorf thinks he will recover." Jackson had been holding his breath, but he began to breathe again.

"I am happy to hear that. Esker is my friend, and I would be grieved to lose him," he said. His fatigue was obvious to Eudora, who was surprised to feel empathy for an Indian.

"I saw you boys filing into town this morning," she said. "You had the town quite stirred up over your disappearance." She paused, almost afraid to ask. "Did you catch the damned things?"

"Yes ma'am," said Jackson. "We fought them. They killed six of our men and stole our horses. We managed to kill a few of them, but most got away." Eudora's shoulders sagged. She looked at Esker and said,

"Those Comanches are meaner than anybody, white, black or red, who lives in this country." She looked Jackson in the eye. "Except for me, maybe." She smiled weakly and offered Jackson some coffee from a pot by the fire.

"I'd like to sit with Esker for a time, if you don't object," he said.

"I would prefer that you should finish your coffee and get back to the barracks," she said. "I shouldn't wonder that the Captain will be waiting for you," she added and smiled stiffly.

CHAPTER 31

Early the next morning, Captain Price rousted Jackson from his cot. All of the men from the 1st Squad had gone home--most of them on foot and grumbling. The men sleeping in the barracks were the 2nd Squad. They had come in during the night and the early morning to begin their rotation. Price told Jackson,

"I need you to help me bargain for some horses," he said. "Maybe the sellers will figure on bargaining since an Indian will come back and steal the horses anyway," he grinned. "Maybe that will make us seem more deserving of charity."

They spent the rest of the morning begging horses from the local populace. Though all the rangers were responsible for their own mounts, Price intended to replace those lost at his own expense. By the end of the day, they had gathered a half dozen fair to middling broomtails and four mules in reasonable condition. Most were on loan from their owners. Jackson was given a horse in fair condition, though he was a little old and had a parrot mouth.

"I do believe he could eat corn through a picket fence," said Price. "You might name him "Buck" on account of being so buck-toothed." Jackson agreed that he was a funny looking horse. He thought the Comanche might even decline stealing him.

The weather warmed and the mud dried. Dust clouds rolled down the streets, and blew under doors and sifted through shingles, vexing those who cared much about housekeeping. They were few. The Captain's view was that dry weather was traveling weather, and told his squad to pack up for patrol.

The 2nd squad was composed of thirteen men. They were by large the oldest men in the Company. Many had fought the Comanche with ranging companies in the 50's, and had served together in one engagement or another. Price thought their age was more than offset by experience. Instead of floppy wool felts or big sombreros, many wore skin hats or caps. The men were generally hairy, and some had greasy beards reaching to their waists. Most of them were singularly dirty and Jackson had seen lice climb along the seams of their filthy garments more than once. So far, he had avoided getting them since Dowdy had given Esker and him new clothes. At night, he rolled his blanket a few yards away from the clustered men.

After a day of greasing rifles and repairing tack, the old men mounted and Price led them back across the Leon. Though they were always on the scout for Comanche, their purpose was to investigate a report of deserters holed up in the thickets along the river. Jackson picked up a trail only six miles north of the settlements. He thought they must have family or friends on a ranch near town who were supplying them. He identified four shod horses, which he judged to be better mounts than the rangers were provided. Price looked forward to appropriating them.

The sun had almost set when they made camp next to the river. Several of the old rangers suffered from rheumatism, and wanted to warm their aches by a fire. Keeping the fire below the river bluff would prevent them from being detected if the deserters were nearby. Three old men occupied most of the space near the fire. Jackson sat as far back as he could. It had been a warm winter day, and its heat had been sufficient for him. He wondered why old people always seemed to be cold. He listened to the men tell their stories.

A man named Jedediah wore a mangy fur cap. An old man asked him why he never removed it from his head; said he wore it both winter and summer. The others chuckled and told Jedediah to show the younger ones his reason for always keeping his head covered. He turned from the fire and removed his cap. He bowed his head low to improve their view. His scalp was not only hairless, but was composed of grisly scar tissue.

"The Kiowa took my har back in '52," he grinned and ran his hand over his waxy pate. "We was rangin' down the San Saba. A baby had been took and we were lookin' for it," he shook his head and lit his pipe. After a minute he said, "We never found the poor thang, just some pieces of it."

"Go on, Jed, and tell the damn story," his friend poked his arm and grinned.

Jedediah continued, "It was morning of the day we started back for the settlements. I had just squatted behind the brush to take my mornin' ease. Now a Kiowa is hell for takin' advantage of a white man when he gets his pants down around his ankles. Took an arrow in my side. They thought I was dead, and so did I, but I weren't. Gritted my teeth so hard I broke one." He pulled the hide of his cheek back to reveal the stub of a molar. The men sat silent in expectation of more story.

"And that was that," he concluded.

The morning dawned gray and Jackson could smell rain. By the time the men had packed and mounted a thin drizzle added to the gloom. Jackson was glad it was not raining harder, since the tracks would be harder to follow. As it was, their quarry had not been careful. They rode their mounts through soft dirt when stony ground could be found a few yards uphill from the river. On their former campsites remained extinguished fires, and garbage. Price caught up with Jackson.

"These boys are not seasoned bandits, I guess."

"No," replied Jackson. "I suppose they just want to stay alive. From their careless manner, I would say they appear to believe they are on a church picnic."

"Well, I hate to interrupt their party, but I reckon the Provost will want to speak with them," said Price.

Jackson found the deserters a few miles upstream. They lounged around a large smoky fire, where they cooked bacon on green sticks. They had not posted a lookout. Their rifles were stacked. Two were old squirrel guns, but two were new Enfields. Jackson mused that the rangers would welcome their addition to the arsenal. Their horses were in good shape as well. He made it out of the brush unseen, and found his ugly horse. The squad was only a mile behind him. He gave his report to Captain Price.

Price directed his men dismount and approach the camp from upstream, downstream and from the bluff above the river. The only avenue of escape was to jump in the river, which was deep at this reach and swift as well. Three of the deserters, shocked to see armed and hairy old men charge into their camp, jumped to their feet and threw their hands in the air. The fourth ran to the stack of arms, and was shot down before he could shoulder the rifle.

"Don't end us, boys!!" screamed a young man with a yellow beard. "We give up!" Jackson gathered the rifles, and stacked them farther from the camp.

Jedediah tied their hands while another brought their horses. "You ain't gonna hang us, are you?" said a boy, who trembled so hard he had to sit down.

"No, son," said Captain Price. "We are going to take you back to Hamerton. The Provost Marshal will be there in a week or so. He will decide what to do with you." They tied the prisoners to their horses and rode back to the barracks, a little more than a day away.

CHAPTER 32

Jackson felt empathy for the prisoners. Like him, they were fleeing the Confederacy, though he thought their reasons were less grounded in honorable philosophical conflict than his own. The setting sun was a smeary red on the horizon when they made the barracks. Having no prison, the rangers locked them in Price's store and posted two guards. Jackson had the first watch. After his second hour, he moved away from the other guard, an old man who had fallen asleep. He whispered to them through a crack in the wall.

"Where did you men serve before you ran?" For a moment, there was no sound, then low muttering. He supposed they were selecting a spokesperson.

"What you wanna know it for?" A raspy voice answered through the crack. Jackson could not see him, but the voice sounded like it belonged to one of the older men.

"Just curious, I suppose," he said. "I wanted to know if you had been in battle or maybe just fled those Galveston mosquitoes."

"All four of us got recruited by McCullough," the voice whispered. "It was gonna be a lark. We were with the 11th Texas Cavalry at the Boston Mountains." After a minute of silence, he added, "They whupped us bad, and killed General McCullough, too."

"Is that why you deserted?" said Jackson.

The voice chuckled. "The goddamn Yankees killed our whole command—all our generals. Before the sons-a-bitches went to their heavenly reward, they saw fit to put us in the field with nothin' to eat. Then it snowed and we had no coats. The whole shebang just fell apart." Jackson heard him move closer to the wall. "We had Cherokee with us. They killed and then scalped dead and wounded alike. Not so sure they didn't scalp one or two of us. The Yankees scattered us with an artillery barrage. We ran till we got separated and lost, but headed generally southwest. We got far enough down the road that goin' back didn't make much sense, I guess."

Gibbons arrived a week after their capture. The weather was bright and cold, and the shackled men shivered for the lack of coats and blinked in the glare. Jackson hid at the corner of Price's store. He noted that Gibbons still wore his ornate pillbox hat.

He dismounted and approached Price. "Good morning, Captain," he said, emphasizing Price's rank. He was himself a Lieutenant, but in the regular army and he thought little of ranks issued in Frontier Organizations. "These, I suppose, are the miscreants?" he said, making a dramatic and open palmed sweep of his hand.

"They are indeed, less the one we shot on the river," said Price.

"What of horses and arms?" said Gibbons. "They are needed for the cause, and needed right quick."

"They were afoot and unarmed," said Price with deadly earnest.

"Now, now, Captain," he sneered. "These men could not have survived without mounts and armament." He closed the gap between himself and Price. He looked up into Price's face, which was at least a head above his. His trim little beard twitched. "I demand the forfeiture of both arms and mounts under the authority of the Confederate States of America!!" he hissed. "Failure to do so is treason, and I will hang you from the nearest tree!!"

Both the second squad, who had not departed, and the third squad who had just begun to arrive, surrounded Gibbons' troops, and outnumbered them two to one. The cocking of rifles and pistols underscored the silence. Gibbons nervously looked around him.

"Those!! Those!!" he pointed. "Those two are Enfield rifles, CSA issue!!" He ran forward and grasped the barrel of one held by Jedediah, the old scout. Jed kicked Gibbons' feet from under him, and he landed on his back in a little puff of dust. He prodded Gibbons with the barrel of the loaded and cocked rifle.

"I reckon you should gather your prisoners and herd them out of town," he said in a whisper. "You got what you come for, now go on."

Gibbons stood up and dusted himself off. His pillbox had fallen to the ground, and its little feather had gotten dirty. He glared at the surrounding men, and then turned to Price.

"This is not the end of the matter. I shall leave you to ponder the dire consequences of your treason." His lower lip trembled so hard he could barely control his speech. "Sergeant McCourty!! Dismount your men and gather these prisoners."

131

McCourty spat into the dust and repeated the orders. Price motioned to three of his men and conferred with them. They left and soon returned with three of the worst mounts in the remuda. Jackson's parrot-mouthed mare was one of them.

"We can't spare saddles, but you are welcome to carry your prisoners on these," said Captain Price. One of the rangers quickly fashioned hackamores from short lengths of rope. Gibbons accepted the horses but did no more than glare at Price.

Jackson watched the men ride off to the north. It was approaching noon, but the winter light was thin. A stiff north wind kicked up dust at the feet of the departing horses. The prisoners looked cold and sad.

"What will they do with them, Captain?" he said.

"Oh, I don't suppose they will hang. They need them for cannon fodder. I reckon they will go back to the war soon enough." He smiled. "In the meantime, they will have to listen to that shrill little rooster all the way back. Might make going back to the war a more inviting proposition."

CHAPTER 33

Eudora was washing Esker's face when he woke. His fever had lasted four days and when it broke he sweated through his blankets. His first sight was her face, which was calm and beautiful. She wasn't young, he thought. But she was not so old that her beauty had faded much. Her mouth was a bow; her eyes were blue and heavy-lidded; her hair was auburn. As she bent over him, a lock of her hair pulled from the gather at the nape of her neck and brushed his face. Her face was close when he opened his eyes.

"Well, there you are," she smiled. "I believe you might just live after all."

Esker smiled weakly.

He was soon able to walk about the cabin, though his weakness surprised him. Eudora fed him daily broth and eggs, and after a few days he had recovered sufficiently to explore the yard. The weather was cold and the sky a brilliant blue. He plunged his hand into the loose soil of her garden. He held the crumbling dirt to his nose and inhaled the fragrance of green things which had yet to be. She surprised him there kneeling before her bed of turnips.

"I can get you a hoe, and you can start work today, if you want," she said.

"I might just do that." He smiled at her. Her face had seen much sun, and in the clear light of the cold day, he could see a faint cluster of freckles across her nose and cheeks. Her hair strayed from under her bonnet and caught the light.

"I have a proposition for you, Mr. Doyle. I need a man to tend to some of the chores around here, and my husband thinks I need one to fend off the Indians. Well, a man or some more dogs, I suppose." She squatted next to Esker and looked him in the eye. "I will give you room and board and two dollars a week. You can room in the smokehouse. It has a stove, and I can make other arrangements for my pork."

"That suits me fine." Then he cleared his throat and said reluctantly, "Well...but once I am healed, I will have to return to rangering ten days a month."

"Very well, then. Ten days a month, you will be Captain Price's concern, and the remaining twenty you shall be mine."

They shook hands on the deal. In a few days, Esker collected his belongings from the barracks and moved into the smokehouse. The room was small and smelled like bacon and live oak smoke. He swept the stone floor and installed an old bedstraw mattress Eudora Carson had discarded. He was eating better than he had in over a year, and his strength returned rapidly. Eudora allowed Jackson to visit him at the smokehouse frequently.

"I don't know if you can return to the troop after living in such luxury," Jackson said as he admired Esker's little room. Esker laughed. "And I suppose you would rather stay here and pine over Mrs. Carson than sleep with a bunch of smelly men." Esker didn't laugh.

He stared at the dusty floor and said, "It ain't so far from the truth, Jackson."

CHAPTER 34

Hair Rope reclined under his buffalo robe and listened to the hiss of the dung fire at the center of his lodge. His wives had tacked its edges down and had stuffed grass between the liner and the wall of the tent. It was warm before the fire, but bitter outside. Three early cold fronts had moved down the plains in succession, bringing with them biting wind but no rain or snow. He had just returned with his hunting party from a trip up the Arkansas River in search of buffalo, but they had only killed an old and irritable bull. They butchered him, but Hair Rope knew the meat was too tough for much other than some soup. He thought he might make a new shield from some of the tough hide, though. Nearly all of the buffalo had moved south into the Texas high plains for the winter, leaving only those too old or lame to make the trip. The band needed to move camp and go where the buffalo were, and now that the soldiers were occupied killing each other, they could easily go to Texas and kill enough to get them through the rest of the winter. He thought they might be able to raid some Texans and take horses while they were there.

After a week of bitter cold, the wind turned south. The weather moderated, and the shadows of white cumulus clouds passed over the prairie, looking like herds of buffalo themselves. Hair Rope lobbied Two Bellies to initiate moving the camp. He agreed.

"I thought you would want to stay in your lodge and have your wife braid your hair," Hair Rope said to Two Bellies. "I had guessed you might be too afraid of the Texans," he sneered.

Two Bellies did not answer, but looked at Hair Rope in a way which let him know he was still in charge of the little band, and that his age had not diminished his physical strength to the extent that he would tolerate insolence. Bitterness still lingered over their disagreement at the battle with the rangers at the two little hills. Two Bellies had done the right thing, he thought, and buried their slain warriors in the right way. Hair Rope had returned with a string of horses and mules. The village celebrated Hair Rope's conquest, but ignored Two Bellies' adherence to the right way of doing things.

The weather stayed mild for the week's journey into the high plains. The scouts soon came back with news of buffalo within fifteen miles of their hunting camp. The herd grazed the long grass in one of the little brakes along the Canadian River. There were only a few hundred, but would be easy to kill since the buffalo were enclosed by the little valley. Hair Rope assembled a party, and the camp moved closer to the herd. The hunters killed forty cows and a few young bulls, just enough meat to last the remainder of the winter. There would be hides enough to replace two of the shabbiest lodges.

Having sufficient provender to survive the winter made the band giddy with relief. They feasted for two days after the hunt. Then the work of jerking meat and preparing hides began in earnest. The women were furiously busy, but the warriors were bored and lounged around the camp in their old buffalo robes. Hair Rope suggested they assemble a raiding party to travel southeast in search of horses. They laid out the plan for Two Bellies. They wanted him to lead the village back to the Territory. The raiding party would travel back north through the Cross Timbers with their spoils and meet him in a month.

Two Bellies thought it would be good to be rid of Hair Rope for a while, and it would benefit the young warriors to practice raiding. Two Bellies retained a few of the youngest warriors for the return home. Hair Rope and his party painted their bodies and rode around the camp, making the war cry; brandishing weapons and stirring their enthusiasm for the adventure ahead. Finally, they rode out of the camp, washed their faces in a little creek and packed away their regalia. In three days they made the escarpment overlooking the Rolling Plains. Red hills and yellow grass rolled out below them. Hair Rope feasted on the view. His band had once lived in this country before they were forced onto the little reservation on the Brazos. It was a small patch of land, and they were told they could not leave it to hunt or to raid. Even though, it had been his country for a while. He smiled.

CHAPTER 35

The party rode southeast for a week, following the Brazos and looking for farms or ranches to raid. They encountered a few abandoned cabins and dugouts, but it was clear the Texans had left long before. Hair Rope's party left the Brazos and turned due south. In a few days, the land changed from rolling prairies to dry hills and buttes. White stone shined along their slopes and at their tops. A few of the warriors raced their ponies to the top of a stony hill to view the surrounding country. Iron Bull, the youngest of their group, dismounted and picked up a few fossilized shells.

"It seems to me an odd thing that there are mussel shells on top of these hills," he said. The others dismounted and picked among the fossils.

"It is because in the times before the people, a great bird once plucked them from the river, and perched on this hill to eat them," said Hair Rope, riding up. "My grandmother told me. She lived in this country, as did her grandmother." The warriors gathered around him. "This country was our own before the Texans pushed us out. I became a warrior here. I think I might come back and take this country again." There were smiles and nods of approval. He turned to Iron Bull. "You were the first to find these. Wrap them up in a skin, and keep them on a cord around your neck. They will help you kill Texans and take horses."

Iron Bull did not respond, but gazed past Hair Rope, into the valley beyond. He pointed his chin. "I see a little wagon trailing some horses."

Below in the valley, Heiner Oltdorf saw the Comanche silhouetted against the winter sky.

"Oh me, Bill," he said to the black man riding beside the wagon. "I fear we are fixin' to have a time of it."

The man slapped the reins spurring his team into a run. He attempted to leave his little horse herd behind for the Indians, but the horses broke into a run as well, traveling in a little knot with the wagon at its center. He peered over his shoulder and saw the Indians descending the hill. He whipped the two mules into a panic no less than his own. The left rear wheel of the wagon caught a rock and splintered. The wagon bounced twice and rolled over. Oltdorf dispassionately watched the ground pass six feet below him and then he landed squarely in a large patch of prickly pear. He heard a bone in his left leg snap as he hit the ground. He crawled back to the overturned wagon box. The mules were following the horses at a dead run, dragging the broken wagon tongue and tack behind them. He reached under the wagon and retrieved his shotgun, ammunition and an old revolver.

The little herd and the team disappeared into a shallow valley. They reemerged on the horizon beyond, still running. Bill wheeled his horse and ran back to Oltdorf, who passed him the loaded shotgun. His hand shook.

"Well, I would much rather be sipping some whiskey in a front of a good fire at home right now. Hell, a cup of water would go well. I am dry as powder." He smiled at Bill. "Now you hold your fire until they come good and close, and be sure to aim." He rummaged through a sack of shot and found less than he had hoped. "We won't have too many opportunities, I think." They crouched behind the wagon box and watched Hair Rope and his warriors approach.

Hair Rope could see the men behind the wagon. He motioned half of his party to take the right flank, and took the remainder to the left. Bill fired both barrels of the shotgun at the first horse. It dropped, screaming and flailing its legs. The unseated warrior leapt onto the back of another horse, startling its rider. Oltdorf passed Bill the pistol, and reloaded the shotgun.

"I am sorry that I got you into this!!" shouted Oltdorf, who noticed that the overturned wagon box was on unlevel ground making the inside accessible. "Let's shimmy under!!"

They dug out gun loops on the far side of the box, and wreaked havoc on the feet and legs of a few horses.

Hair Rope signaled his warriors to withdraw. Once they were out of range, he said, "That old white man is bald and ugly, and the black man has hair like a buffalo's. Those scalps are no good. We will go gather those horses instead."

The party raced after the horse herd and disappeared beyond the valley. When Oltdorf and Bill finally squeezed from under the wagon, a cloud of dust on the far horizon was the only indication the Comanche were anywhere near.

"Well, hell, Bill," Oltdorf slumped against the wagon box holding his broken leg in both hands. Bill tore his own shirt into rags and splinted Oltdorf's leg.

"I'll walk on now," said Bill, looking in the direction the Indian's had left. "I'll find some help and come back."

"See that you do," grunted Oltdorf, who had just begun to feel the pain of his shattered leg. "Take the shot gun and the shot. I will keep the pistol, I guess."

Bill said, "Maybe I can find my horse. It will be quicker that way."

The Comanche had ridden southeast which was unfortunately the only direction Bill knew to go to find help. The prairie was rocky, and broken by little creeks and ravines which he followed as long as they tended generally south. On the open prairies, he feared he would be vulnerable to discovery. Bill Smith had belonged to Oltdorf for almost twenty years. He had only been whipped once, but Oltdorf had sold his wife and daughter. At the crest of each hill, he looked north, and considered the possibility of escape, making the Territory, or any place not a slave state. He decided he might do so after he found Oltdorf help. On the second day, he changed his mind and turned north for a few miles. Bill crested a hill and pondered. He didn't know why he would want to help, but it was against his nature to walk away from a wounded man, slave holder or not. It would be easy to slip away from a rescue party at night, anyway.

On his fourth day afoot, a cold wind began to blow from the north, where the sky had taken on a blue-black color. Cold air always looked heavy to him. He had been shirtless since tying up Oltdorf's leg. For all of his desire to be helpful, he wished that he had kept his shirt and used Heiner's instead. He did not want to risk a fire which the Indians might see, but by nightfall, cold and a gale-driven sleet storm left him little choice. He lay with his back to the windward side of a shallow cutbank, and built a fire which reflected its heat against the thick white gravel.

He shivered for several hours until merciful sleep overtook him. He dreamed he was in his bed in the little cabin Oltdorf kept for him, covered in old flour sacks and a wool blanket. In his dream, he had gone from sweet warmth to being uncomfortably hot. In his dream, he struggled to pull his blanket off, but it would not budge. He began to scorch. He awoke. Hair Rope stood on the other side of a fire he had banked next to Bill, and was adding branches to it. Bill's hair and breeches caught fire and he screamed for a while until a lance finally silenced him. Hair Rope rolled him out of the smoking crevasse and cut his fingers off as a trophy, and rolled them in a little piece of hide. They had captured Oltdorf's horses, and were on their way northeast toward the Cross Timbers. He judged the weather to be of the type which would linger for a while. It was time to go home.

Oltdorf had waited under the wagon for the storm to pass. It cut the wind and sleet, but he had no blankets. The next day, he crawled from under the wagon. The clouds held, but the sleet had stopped and the wind had calmed. Hourly, he propped himself up and looked southeast. There was no Bill and no rescue party, but fortunately, no Indians either. Another good fortune was that the water barrel had not shattered when the wagon overturned, so he did not fear dying of thirst. Wolves had bothered him some and each night their number increased and they came a little closer. He had retreated under the wagon before each sunset, but watched them watching him each day. His leg had begun to blacken and smell. He knew it would have to come off, but that would be a problem to contend with only if he made it to the settlements. It worried him.

"One exigency at a time, Heiner," he muttered.

He lost consciousness once in a while, and the rest of the time he was in a fever fog. The pain in his leg had subsided, but the black streaks had moved all the way to his hip. He had rolled to his side, studying his leg when he saw three Indians on horseback descending the hill east of his inverted wagon, which he had named Fort Oltdorf. He cocked his pistol, not knowing if it was wiser to shoot himself or take a shot at the Indians.

Whirlwind saw a man at the corner of the overturned wagon aiming a pistol at him. He raised his hand and hailed him. He pointed his lips at Oltdorf, and motioned the two riders to follow him. "It is a white man and his little cart," he said to them. They carefully held their hands away from their sides and their weapons. Whirlwind dismounted and slowly approached Oltdorf, speaking softly and smiling, until he saw his rotting leg. He grimaced; pointed at Oltdorf's wound. "That is a bad wound," he said.

"I don't know what you're sayin' but if you are inquiring about my leg, it hurts like hell and stinks like a son-of-a-bitch," said Oltdorf. "I don't suppose you have any whiskey, do you?"

Whirlwind gathered sage and with a kettle from Oltdorf's wagon, prepared a tea. While the tea steeped, the three men discussed his prognosis.

Elk wrinkled his nose. "That old white man is rotten."

"I think he will die soon," Eats Little said behind his hand.

"Well, I think I will stay with him until he dies. Maybe I can wrap that leg in sage. It will not cure him, but it might keep the smell away, I think," said Whirlwind.

CHAPTER 36

The first squad had assembled for patrol. Esker was sufficiently recovered to join the troop again, though the arrow head, still embedded by his spine, poked him painfully when he breathed deeply. His first night back, he was joshed and teased mercilessly about his living with Eudora Carson. Esker was embarrassed and angry, feared that he might be expected to stand up for her reputation with his fists.

Sgt. Mosey took his arm and led him aside. "Now, Esker, them boys was just joshin'. Tryin' to get your ire up." Esker gave him a dead-pan glare.

Mosey laughed, "You do have a case of it, don't you boy?"

Esker was in love with Eudora. His attention to chores was compromised by his need to gaze on her. But Eudora had shown no signs of reciprocation. She smiled at him often, but never held eye contact long enough to encourage him. Making it worse, it was obvious to him that she knew he was in love with her. She laughed when he looked at her with moony eyes. She wrote letters to her husband frequently, and read aloud to Esker those which she had received from him when they were not too personal. Albert Sydney had been in no life-threatening conflicts other than attacks by mosquitoes, and the only military action had been a fracas on the Sabine, and then he had only watched as the Union ships sailed upriver.

Esker was glad to get away from his chores and the pangs of unrequited love, though. He was glad to be back with Jackson and the rough men with their crude senses of humor.

Jackson was especially glad of his recovery and was gentler with his feelings. "It is to be expected that you would have feelings for your nurse," he said. "It has been a long time since a woman has taken care of you." Esker ducked his head a little in embarrassment and said,

"She is the first woman who ever really talked to me. Maw was good to me, but she had little to say."

The squad started their patrol on a clear winter day. Esker noted the sky was the color of a robin's egg; felt relief and even joy at being on the range again. Their route was generally northwest, which soon took them into a hilly and pleasant country. The prairie was graced by scattered live oaks mottes, which made for good places to camp and noon. Deer were especially abundant, and the men ate better than when they were at home. The patrol had taken on the atmosphere of a holiday, when Jackson, who scouted several miles beyond the squad, picked up the trail of a Comanche raiding party. They rode mainly shoeless horses, but the little herd they drove was shod. Their trail led a little east of north.

The men were nooning under a live oak grove, and were reluctant to interrupt their dinner. Captain Price gave them a hard look from under his abundant eyebrows, and they began to pack.

"Boys, make sure your armaments are in good working order, I don't want you fiddling with them should we encounter the Indians," he said. "It would be an embarrassment not to be prepared."

By mid-afternoon, the north sky took on an ominous color. Captain Price took advantage of the presence of the abundant mottes, and directed the men to make camp in preparation for a storm.

"It's going to blow for a little while. That cloud appears to have some sleet in it."

The storm blew itself out early the following morning, though it was cold and windy. Before sunrise, Jackson left the men under their blankets and saddled his horse. He knew the raiding party had to stop for the weather, but would start again as soon as possible. The ground was slick with sleet and ice, but the wind would soon dry it up.

CHAPTER 37

Jackson had been on the trail for most of the day. The troop lagged miles behind. He thought it likely that they were reluctant to leave their fires. The trail was easy to follow, but it was a few days old. He thought the Comanche were likely back in the Territory by now.

Jackson smelled the odor of smoke on the wind, which blew in cold and stiff from the north. It was not long before he spotted a smudge of greasy black smoke rising from a little creek channel. As he approached, he recognized the scent of burned man. He found Bill where the Comanche had left him. Varmints had been at him some. It was clear he had suffered much before he died.

He piled rocks over the corpse and left a rock cairn on the creek bank should anyone care to find him. He followed the trail until he discovered another, running in the opposite direction. The more recent turned northeast and the older ran almost due south. Given his discovery and therefore the possibility that he would find other victims, he followed the older trail. By mid-morning, he again smelled smoke, but this time from a wood fire. He dismounted and followed a gully to its head at the top of a ridge. He peered over its edge. The wind kicked dust into his eyes. He slid down the slope, and once he cleared it, he returned and saw an overturned wagon, and a white man lying on the ground surrounded by three Indians. He had his Sharp's, and considered trying to shoot them. The shot was a long one, so he scooted on his belly, and repositioned himself in a ravine closer to his targets. As he sighted his rifle, he heard the Indians speaking. He heard

Kickapoo words. He crawled out of the ravine, and in Kickapoo, shouted that he was a friend. The Indians turned from the fire. Jackson immediately recognized Whirlwind and then the two men who had rescued their party from Gibbons at the river below the escarpment.

Whirlwind smiled in recognition. The others were reserved, but showed no alarm.

"I see you have lost your white man hair," said Whirlwind, picking up one of Jackson's braids. "I guess maybe you decided to be a Kickapoo again, but these look like Comanche braids."

Whirlwind was making a joke, but it hit a tender spot. "You have the long braids as well, though I would never call you a Comanche." Whirlwind winced.

"I am glad to see you again. Are you going to take this white man's hair?" Jackson smiled. "Does not look like he has much to take."

Whirlwind knelt by Oltdorf. "This old man is sick. He has a black leg, and it stinks. I don't think he will live long."

Oltdorf awoke. "Damned if I ain't a magnet for Indians." His voice was weak and low. "Where did this one come from?"

"I am a scout for the Price Company, ranging out of Hamerton County," said Jackson. "The troop should catch up shortly." He sat next to Oltdorf. "Did the Comanches catch you?"

"I am glad to hear English. This bunch has been jabberin' at me. I don't speak Indian," he whispered. "They catched me, to answer your question," said Oltdorf. "Ran off with my horses. I turned this wagon over runnin' from them, and broke my damned leg." He looked around. "You didn't run into my nigra, Bill, did ya?"

"Yes. I buried him this morning," said Jackson.

"Well ... Mercy," he sighed. "That is a shame. Bill was a good man, as good as any man I know," he said.

Jackson turned to Whirlwind. "You are a long way from your river today," he said.

"We are going northwest to catch Na-Koh-Aht and his people coming south from the Territory. They are going to live in Mexico and be Kickapoo again. Maybe you should come too."

Jackson had long considered Whirlwind's former invitation, but it was unthinkable to abandon his responsibility to the troop, especially when they were in the field. "I get to kill more Comanche if I stay. Maybe I will come after we whip them all."

"A warrior must do what he thinks is right," said Whirlwind, "but a white man must do what others tell him to do. I think we will go now. All Indians look alike to the whites. They might think we are enemies."

The men mounted and Jackson watched them disappear in the distance. He turned his attention to Oltdorf, who had expired while he had exchanged pleasantries. He rolled him in a wagon sheet and waited for the troop.

CHAPTER 38

Lieutenant Gibbons kicked the remains of a campfire. There were over a hundred little patches of charred grass where the Indians had made their little cooking fires. They had cooked their food with buffalo dung — bois d'vac — since there were no trees in sight. Sergeant McCourtey supervised the exhumation of a small grave. He called to Gibbons. The corpse of a small child, a girl, lay beside the grave. The burial was recent.

"Well, we can be sure this was no captive, Lieutenant, unless an Indian captive, and we don't give much of a shit about them, now do we?" said McCourtey. "Comanche and Kiowa don't bring their babies along on raids. I think this bunch is peaceful."

"I know no peaceful Indians within the boundaries of the state of Texas," replied Gibbons. "From the look of all of these cooking fires, I estimate there are a thousand or more. A thousand Indians of any species is a threat to the state's safety and sovereignty."

Gibbons thrilled at the prospect of glory. He imagined himself leading a glorious cavalry charge against an enemy more than anything. It was his destiny. It was a right they cheated him of when they assigned him to Provost duty on the godforsaken frontier. He imagined the promotions, plaudits and admiration, not to mention the favorable attention of the ladies.

They mounted and followed the trail south. It was almost a half mile wide, scarred by the dragging of travois. The weather was uncertain and turning cold. Gibbons decided to break for the settlements, and alert the rangers.

CHAPTER 39

The patrol retrieved Heiner Oltdorf's corpse. One ranger, a distant cousin, had insisted that they bring the body back for burial in the family cemetery. They had spent an afternoon attempting to right and repair the wagon for use as a hearse, but it was too damaged. Esker volunteered to carry the body behind the pommel of his saddle. Oltdorf had been a small man, and he would fit easily.

"I would not feel right about bein' that close to a dead man for so long," said Corporal Woodrow. "I reckon he might get too comfortable with me and want to crawl into my blankets at night."

"You would be lucky to get even a haint to bed with you, Woodrow," said Jedediah. "You are uglier than most've the corpses I seen."

"I ain't superstitious. His rotten leg does give him an odor, but he has not yet begun to turn," observed Esker.

This lead to a long discussion about the process of decomposition, and the various states of horror it achieved. The conversation lasted most of the day. The troop concluded it was best to avoid it, if one could manage.

They made the upper reaches of the Lampasas River by the second day. Jackson spotted a party of riders traveling a course parallel to their own and several miles distant. He assumed they were white men, as they rode hunched over in their saddles. Captain Price sent Jackson and Sergeant Mosey to investigate.

Jackson recognized Lt. Gibbons at half a mile. He thought Gibbons must have recognized him, too, since the patrol started for them at a gallop.

"Arrest that man!" Gibbons shouted and pointed his pistol at Jackson. "This is the so called Cherokee scout who ambushed us at the Paluxy River!"

His horse danced with excitement as he shouted. Sergeant McCourtey and his men pulled Jackson from his horse and bound his hands. Gibbons dismounted and walked slowly to Jackson. He peeled off his riding gloves, crossed his arms across his chest and then rested against the pommel of his sword.

"I told you to consider the inevitable day when the full force of justice would be upon you." He was enjoying himself.

Mosey sat his horse and watched the proceedings impassively. "What did he do?"

"He attacked this very patrol on the Paluxy River! Claimed he was a Cherokee scout in the service of the Confederate States!"

Mosey sucked his teeth and looked back toward the squad, which had turned and was now approaching.

"Well, I guess I don't know what kind of Indian he is, but he is our scout, and I reckon we still have use for him."

Captain Price recognized Gibbons at a distance by his pillbox hat. He let out a long sigh.

"That little rooster is back."

"What is it now, Gibbons?" Price said, as he rode up.

"This man was with a party of Indians and a white man who attacked us on the Paluxy River," said Gibbons. His voice was shrill and he was not at all happy to see Price. His face was flushed, and at the sight of Price, his little chin beard began to tremble.

Esker hung to the rear of the column, but Gibbons spotted him. "That man!! That man at the rear!! He was one of them." Gibbons was jubilant.

Esker rode forward. Price appraised him for a moment. "When did this happen?" he asked Gibbons.

"A year ago last September. We counter-attacked, but the cowards out ran us," he lied. "Now it is our duty to hang these men at the earliest convenience."

Price shook his head. "I am afraid you are mistaken, Lieutenant. These men have been with this troop for at least two years, and never far out of my sight." He stared Gibbons in the eye without blinking. "Untie my scout, or I will have you and your men arrested." The squad encircled Gibbons's little patrol. He was surrounded again. His shoulders sagged. "I will see to it that you are court-martialed," he hissed. "This is not over!"

McCourtey untied Jackson's wrists. Gibbons wanted to countermand the order, but stayed furiously silent in the midst of so many armed adversaries. He then remembered his mission. It brightened his mood a little. His swagger returned.

"Captain, for now, I have more important matters to attend to," he said. "I will deal with those," he pointed at

Jackson and Esker "at a more convenient time." He mounted his horse so he could be eye-level with Price. "There is a band of hostile Indians, perhaps a thousand, moving south two days ride from here. You and your men will join forces with this patrol, and all other militia and troops we can muster, to intercept and engage them. This shall be my command, and the Frontier Organizations will follow my orders without debate." Price smiled at him in an infuriating way. Gibbons blanched.

Jackson, rubbing his wrists, spoke up, "Captain, those are Kickapoo. They are just trying to get to Mexico. They are peaceful. They have women and children with them. Most of them are farmers, Christians too."

"Is that so, Lieutenant?" said Price.

"There are no peaceful tribes known within the borders of the state," said Gibbons. "We shall engage and eradicate them."

CHAPTER 40

Two Bellies' hunting party saw the long train of Kickapoo moving south. The throng stretched almost a mile. There were men, women, children, dogs, travois and wagons. There was also a large horse herd. Two Bellies did not think much of Kickapoo. They rarely fought, and when they did they did so poorly, he thought. But this time, there were more than could be counted, and he did not think his hunting party had much of a chance of killing some without great risk to his warriors. If the Kickapoo kept a poor guard, though, they might be able to steal some horses at night. He decided to follow them for a while, keeping a hill or two between them for cover.

Though he did not like him, Two Bellies had to confess that Hair Rope was a talented horse thief. He was able to enter a horse herd without detection by either the guards or the horses. He simply walked into a herd and left with a dozen or more. Two Bellies reluctantly concluded that he should have taken him on this trip.

On the third night following the Kickapoo, a warrior named Iron Hawk and another named Broken Arm crept into their sleeping camp. Iron Hawk was almost as old as Two Bellies, but had kept his skills honed. Broken Arm was Iron Hawk's protégé, and accompanied him for a lesson in stealing horses. The night was half finished, and a little fingernail moon was setting. It gave just enough light to negotiate the rough ground and see the horses clearly, but not enough to easily reveal two figures skulking in the darkness. They lay in the grass a few yards from the first line of picketed horses. At first, the horses noticed them and became restless. After a few minutes, they calmed and began chewing at the grass at their feet. Others slept.

Iron Hawk crawled closer, and let the horses get his scent. He stood, and began stroking the nearest horse. She snuffed at him and he let her get her nose full, but the horse showed no skittishness when he untied her from the picket line. He led the horse to Broken Arm, who waited in the brush. He returned twice more, each time bringing a horse back. They took the horses back to the little thicket where their own were tied and then herded the horses back to Two Bellies' camp. The warriors were elated, and the other young men wanted to take horses, too.

"There will be time," said Two Bellies. "We will follow for a few more days. With that many horses, if we take only a few each night, it might be a while before they discover them missing and increase the horse guard."

CHAPTER 41

The squad and their mounts looked like men and horses molded from dust by the time they reached Hamerton. Esker and Jackson accompanied Oltdorf and his kin to a little cemetery along Cowhouse Creek. Oltdorf had begun to turn by the time they reached familiar ground, and Esker had felt a little queasy for the past twenty miles. They quickly buried him in a wagon sheet, and Oltdorf's kin left to inform the family.

When they reached town the ranger barracks were a beehive. The relief squad had arrived, and theirs, the relieved, were changing horses and riding out. The Captain hailed them.

"I need you to ride up into Erath to let them know the Minutemen are required. The rest of the boys are scattering likewise to pass the news."

Esker was disappointed. He could think of little other than getting back to his comfortable little shed, so he could watch Eudora through her kitchen window. Jackson saw the look on his face and grinned at him.

"I suppose, Esker, we should get fresh mounts and lope up there, don't you think?"

Esker grunted.

They rode north and east for two days, through sere prairies dotted with the green of live oak, and then into scrubby and bare-limbed post oak forest. A resident of the first settlement they encountered sat on the porch of a little dog run cabin and stared blankly at them.

Esker sat his horse before the porch rail and said, "Mister, we are rangers with the Jim Price Company, and we have been sent up here to muster the Minutemen to help us engage a party of Indians to our west."

The man had a large chaw in his cheek, and was intently working it from cheek to cheek into a manageable wad, a thing which seemed to require all of his attention. He finally spat a long stream of tobacco juice, and looked at them as though he had just become aware of their presence.

"Well. I reckon we have such about here, but you will have some struggle a-findin' them, as they are, ary one of 'em, out to a cow hunt," said the man, who had not blinked since they arrived.

Jackson said, "Where is the cow hunt? I suppose we will have to go out and round them up."

The man raised his eyebrows in surprise. "You mean you goin' ta round up the cattle, too?"

"No sir," replied Esker. We want to find the Minutemen and herd them back to Hamerton."

"Oh. Well, they are where the cows are, I suppose, though I do not know where that might be," said the man, who spat another brown stream.

After some slow negotiation, they arranged for the man to guide them to the spots likely to yield the cow hunters. When they found them, they seemed equally slow in speech and manner, but agreed to muster at Hamerton as soon as they had gathered their stock.

Esker and Jackson saw the gray dust cloud over Hamerton long before they even reached the high ground above town. Ranger troops and militia from the frontier counties had converged on the settlement, more than tripling its population overnight and stirring up more dust than was usual. Dozens of wagons, horses and even a mountain howitzer on a carriage choked the streets. Butternut uniforms of State Troops were sprinkled among the variously clothed and ragged populace. Men crowded the doors of the saloons, waiting their turn to occupy the bar for a few minutes. More than a few had already occupied the bar, and lay like dead men beneath the pecan trees along the creek. Onlookers stood at the edge of the activity, amazed to see so many people they did not know.

Jackson reported to Captain Price, who was impatient with the slowness of the Erath company.

"Sometimes, one must just leave the cows to fend for themselves," he said. "If it had not been for the danged farmers running home to plant, Travis might not have lost the Alamo," he said.

He instructed Jackson to gather three of the first squad and scout the location of the Indians. "You can sleep first," he said. "Then change mounts and go in the morning."

"Captain. These are Kickapoo, my own people. I know some of them, and can attest that they are just passing through. They have their children with them, for God's sake."

"Well, I suppose the matter will be clear even to Gibbons when we catch up with them," said Price. If what you say is true, only a crazy man would pick a fight with that many," He placed his hand on Jackson's arm. "We need you with us. We need an interpreter so we can clear this up. It is in their interest as well as ours."

Esker looked for Eudora in the crowd of onlookers. Not finding her there, he loped out of town to her cabin, loosed his horse and ran up the stairs. She met him at the door.

"My goodness, Esker, I thought there was an elephant running up my steps," she laughed. When she laughed, her face shone like the sun. The sound was the best music to Esker, who grinned wordlessly at her. She wiped her hands on her dish towel and looked him over. "I do believe I could grow a mess of turnips in all that dirt stuck to you." She took him by the hand and led him into the kitchen. She stuck a biscuit in his free hand and poured him a cup of coffee.

"I am awfully glad to be home," he said. "I had to carry a dead man all the way from the head of the Lampasas to a little cemetery southwest of town." He looked at the biscuit in his dirty hands. "He stunk after a while."

"I'll pull the tub inside and fill you a bath," she said. "I don't know if it's you or the dead man, but I confess you do have a whang to you."

Esker sat in the tub until the water turned cold. Eudora handed him a piece of sacking to dry on. She averted her eyes until he had covered himself. He sat down on her kitchen chair. She unfolded another towel and began drying his hair. His shoulders drooped, and he leaned into her.

"Esker, I do believe you had too little mothering," she said without teasing. "I'd vow you need a woman to keep you for a while."

"My maw died spring eighteen months ago. My two brothers and my paw as well," he said. "Vigilantes hung the three of 'em in the the front yard of my house, and they raped my mother to death."

Eudora pulled up a chair and sat in front of him. She took his hand. "Who would do such a terrible thing, Esker?"

"My family were Lincolnites, out in east Texas. I guess the vigilantes thought they might spy for the Union, though it makes no sense. They were just farmers. The same vigilantes killed our pastor, too. He raised Jackson. Jackson worked for him, I suppose."

"And I suppose you aren't Confederate, then," she said, dropping his hand.

"We ain't much of nothin' now. Just Rangers."

A gentle knock came at the door. Eudora stood, gazed on Esker for a moment, then left the room. When she returned, Jackson followed her.

"Esker. We have orders to scout those Kickapoo tomorrow. We will leave in the morning as soon as it is light enough to see."

CHAPTER 42

By late morning, Jackson, Esker, Sergeant Mosey and Corporal Woodrow had cleared the lime rock country and were riding across rolling prairies. Jackson had less than usual to say about the country they were traveling through, which surprised Esker. New land always excited him. Esker joined him at the head of the little column. Mosey and Woodrow dozed in their saddles.

"You appear out of sorts, this morning," said Esker.

"I don't want this mission," whispered Jackson. He looked at Esker, his expression grave. "These traveling people we are supposed to scout are Kickapoos. Some are the same who fed and guided us over a year ago."

"You mean Joe Blue Bill and Whirlwind?! They are in that bunch?"

"I don't know if Blue Bill is, but I saw Whirlwind and the two warriors who saved us from the patrol on that shallow little river. They were caring for Oltdorf until the squad caught up. They were traveling to catch up with them. They are all going to Mexico to get away from bad whites and the Comanche. That is all they want. They are not hostile."

"God almighty, Jackson! Gibbons intends to kill the lot of 'em!" he said too loud, rousing Mosey and Woodrow.

Mosey rode up next to Esker. "I heard what you said, Jackson. You mean to tell me we have the whole damned country out to attack a peaceful bunch? I heard Gibbons say they were Comanche. These are Kickapoo? Your own people?"

"They are. I suspect most of them are women and children. War parties do not travel with their families."

"What do you propose, Jackson? I don't intend to take part in a massacre of a bunch of women and babies," said Esker.

"I intend to warn them," said Jackson.

Corporal Woodrow said, "Hells Bells, Mosey! Gibbons will have ever one of us hanged, goddamnit! I ain't havin' no part in this," he spat into the dust.

"Woodrow," said Mosey. "We don't want to slit your throat and leave you out here for the critters to scatter," he said, baring his teeth at the Corporal. "I believe you have a bad case of the drizzles. Soldier's complaint, you know. We are not so far away that you can't turn back. Go tell Price we rode on without you. But if you tell a soul, I vow I will gut you before they hang me."

Corporal Woodrow considered the proposition. He never expected his friend to turn traitor, and he never expected him to threaten him. "Well, I'll be," he said. He turned his horse and rode away. His feelings were hurt.

"If you say a word about this, Woodrow, I'll gut you," Mosey called after him. Woodrow did not look back, just stuck a hand in the air as a gesture of departure.

Esker said, "Well. We could just tell Price and them that those Indians are someplace they ain't."

"There are at least four Tonkawa scouts with the other troops. They would discover the lie before they got four miles west," said Jackson. "Warning them may be the best we can do. At least they can decide how they will respond, I guess."

CHAPTER 43

Corporal Woodrow rode slowly east, while he nursed his hurt feelings and confusion.

"Dang it, Mosey!" he said to his horse, a good one, taken from the deserters. "I never thought you could be so contrary. "Dang it! Dang the lot of 'em."

From a high swell in the prairie, Two Bellies and his warriors watched his slow progress along the trail following a dry creek bed. They had taken half a dozen horses over a period of several nights before the Kickapoo had discovered their loss and doubled the horse guard. They were in route home when they saw the lone rider in the swale a mile below.

"He looks like he is talking to himself," said Broken Arm. "You think maybe he is crazy?"

"He might be," said Two Bellies. "His horse is not, though. That is a better horse than most whites ride. He has more guns than most whites carry."

"I would like to have that horse and those guns," said Iron Hawk, who rode up to watch with them.

Two Bellies who was a little jealous of Iron Hawk's ability to steal horses said, "You always want more horses."

Iron Hawk looked at Two Bellies as though he had spoken nonsense. "I will tell you when I have too many. Maybe that day I will give you one."

The three left the little horse herd to the care of the youngest warriors and rode down the hill to intersect Woodrow, who was so preoccupied with his hurt feelings that he hadn't bothered to notice his surroundings. An arrow hit his left shoulder, nearly lifting him from his saddle. He kicked his horse into a run and quirted him until it was frothing. Two Bellies emptied his pistol at Woodrow until the last shot hit him in the neck. He landed hard on his back, conscious, but paralyzed. He heard the thrum of the hoof beats of his departing horse, and then the footsteps of the warrior as he approached. He could see the toes of his high moccasins. Broken Arm smiled at him, then sat on his chest and scalped him. Then he drove his lance into Woodrow's chest, pinning him to the ground. When he tried to withdraw the lance, it would not budge. He stepped on Woodrow's chest and twisted it. The lance broke halfway up the haft. He shrugged and left it.

When Two Bellies returned with Iron Hawk and Woodrow's horse, he disemboweled him and moved his arms and legs around into a silly pose. This led to a discussion about variations in ridiculous poses, and after making the corpse more flexible by breaking its arms and legs, they were satisfied that it was sufficiently humiliated.

Two Bellies thought it was unusual for a white man to be traveling alone so far from the settlements. He also thought it was likely that the man had been part of a larger party. He decided that they should move into some cover and watch the trail for a few days. If the party was not too large, he thought, they might be able to get more horses and rifles. They had plenty of food, and if needed, they could butcher one of the horses. They found a deep and narrow canyon a few miles from the trail. Its steep sides were covered with scrubby cedar, and a little spring-fed creek flowed through it. It would be good shelter from any weather the winter sent them, and their fires could not be seen at night.

CHAPTER 44

Jackson picked up the trail of the Kickapoo the morning after Woodrow's departure, if one could call it a trail. It was as wide as the Republic Road Esker and Jackson had used to flee east Texas. Wagon ruts and travois tracks disturbed the ground so much it looked like a very long and narrow plowed field.

They found the camp late in the afternoon. They dismounted and hunkered on a rise about a quarter mile from camp, far enough away to avoid intrusion and close enough to be seen. The smokes of hundreds of little cook fires rose from the wooded creek valley below them. Little wickiups had been fashioned from cedar boughs and bark. Women cooked at the fires, and children played between the huts. Jackson said it might be dangerous to just ride into the camp unannounced, so they sat in the fading afternoon light until they were discovered.

Four riders came out to meet them. Jackson had hoped that Whirlwind or one of the others he knew would be in the group, but he recognized no one. Jackson, Mosey and Esker kept their seats, and kept their hands where the approaching Indians could see them.

"What do you want?" shouted one of the riders in English. His hair was cut at jaw length like that of Joe Blue Bill, and he wore a red blanket across his shoulders, but he was otherwise dressed in white man's clothes.

Jackson stood and walked forward. "We have news," he said in Kickapoo. "Do you know Whirlwind? He wants to talk to us."

The warrior turned to the other riders. One rode forward. "I know him. You wait here, and I will bring him to you."

It was well past sunset when Whirlwind arrived. He dismounted and sat facing Jackson. "What do you want?" he said. "Have you given up on being a white man? Have these white men given up on being white men?"

Jackson did not respond to the teasing, and his expression told Whirlwind that the news was bad. "The rangers are bringing soldiers and militia to fight you," he said.

"How many will come?" said Whirlwind. "Are they bringing cannons?"

"I think there will be three or four hundred. I saw one little cannon in Hamerton. The man who is causing this is the man who tried to arrest us on the river."

Whirlwind laughed. "He reminds me of a prairie chicken dancing," he said. "Why would he interfere with us? We have done nothing to the Texans."

"He hates Indians, and he wants to be famous, I think. Some of the soldiers and rangers know that this is a peaceful camp, but they have been given orders," Jackson said.

Whirlwind scratched his head and smiled. "That is something I have never understood about the whites. We make our own decisions. If a warrior decides to fight, he fights.

If he decides to stay at home, he stays at home. White men always want someone to run them."

"They are coming," said Jackson. "I think maybe in two or three days. We are supposed to report where your camp is. The best you can do is talk to them. Send a woman out who speaks English. But be ready to fight."

"Do white men run you??" Whirlwind stood. "You are going to lead them to us?"

"Yes," said Jackson. "They have another three or four Tonkawa scouts who will if I don't. Your trail is pretty clear, anyway," he gestured to the scarred earth leading to their camp.

Whirlwind mounted. "I am sorry you have decided to be a white man. You can leave, but the next time I see you, you will be my enemy."

On the second day of the return trip, Esker noticed a large black lump by the creek the trail followed. He soon realized it was a flock of buzzards feeding on a carcass. Curious, he fired a pistol at the mass of black wings. The buzzards flapped and landed a few feet away.

"Jackson!!" he shouted, and then vomited down the flank of his horse.

"Oh my dear lord," mumbled Mosey. He stood, shaking his head and looking at what little was left of Corporal Woodrow. "I guess the Comanche got him," he snuffled. "And there was me, last thing I said to him was a rudeness."

They dug a grave next to the corpse and scraped the little bit into it.

"Did he have family?" said Esker. "I never knew."

"No." said Mosey. "None that I knew of. The troop was most like it, I suppose."

"Well, I swan," said Esker, who kicked a little more dirt on the grave.

Two Bellies and his warriors watched the rangers bury their friend. Broken Arm said, "Let's go down and take their horses."

"I think it would be better to follow them for a while," said Two Bellies.

CHAPTER 45

Jackson spotted the dust from the westering column miles before they could see the column itself. The dust stood in relief against a distant blue-black sky signaling impending cold and maybe snow. The wind turned furtively to the north, then south again. After a few hours, they saw the column crest of a hill east of them. Gibbons and the regulars rode at its head, flying the Stars and Bars and the 2nd Frontier District pennant. Gibbons had found extra gold braid for his uniform, which flashed in the weak sunlight.

"Well, I'll be. They got all dressed up for the occasion," said Sergeant Mosey, who was easily impressed by pageantry.

"What will we tell them about Woodrow?" said Esker, as they cantered toward the troops.

Jackson said, "Just tell them he had dysentery and had turned back. The Comanche got him. At least the latter is true."

Gibbons saw the scouts and galloped toward them, the standard bearers following. Captain Price saw them too, and wanted to insert himself between Gibbons and Jackson, in case the former still had any intentions of arresting the latter.

"What is your report, scout?!" Gibbons shouted as his mare slid to a sideways stop.

"Well, sir. The Kickapoo are three days out on a little creek not far from the Concho River," said Jackson. "There are close to a thousand encamped, but more than half are women and children. They are peaceful, Lieutenant. There is no indication at all that they are hostiles."

"I did not ask you for your opinion, scout," he looked down his nose at Jackson. "I know you! You are the man subject to arrest after we finish this skirmish," he said between clenched teeth, and that one," he pointed at Esker, his dander was up and his face flushed. "Who sent these men on scout?!"

"I did," said Price, who was riding up. "These are the best scouts I have. I would consider anything they told me to be a fact."

"Two of your so-called scouts are bushwhackers. That Indian just implied that when we attack, we will be murdering women and children. I believe he is just protecting his savage allies. Perhaps those who ambushed my patrol on the Paluxy," said Gibbons.

Price looked at his scouts. "You had four when you left. Where is Corporal Woodrow?"

Mosey kicked his horse forward. "Dead, Captain. Woodrow turned back for the settlements because of the dysentery, sir. Not much more than a day after we set out. We found him on the back trail. The Comanche got him. We buried what was left of him at a little creek along the trail." Mosey looked grieved, and he was. Woodrow had been friend and fellow for many years.

"I regret to hear this," said Price. "He was a good man and will be missed."

"Yessir, he was, and he will be," said Mosey, who wiped his eye with the back of his hand.

Esker nodded in agreement and said, "Well, I vow that he was always kind to me, though I didn't know him well."

"Let's conclude this palaver and be on our way. Captain, if you trust this Indian to scout, he can join the Tonkawas. Otherwise, put these other men back in the ranks," Gibbons said, and loped off with his standard bearers to the head of the column.

The sky had turned a leaden gray, and the wind began blowing in earnest from the northwest. Some of the men had neither blankets nor coats, and put on all of the clothes they had brought with them. There was much borrowing and trading of shirts and slickers as well, and the business slowed the troops down, much to Gibbons' irritation. He rode up and down the ranks, scolding the men.

"Lord, it will be a week before this bunch makes the Concho," said Mosey as they followed behind. Esker grunted and pulled an oil cloth slicker over his head, his only foul weather gear. The column rode into the wind which blew in their faces part of the time and their right ears the rest of the time. Mosey had pulled mattress ticking from his bed for such an occasion, and loaded both ears with it.

"I was prone to ear aches as a boy," he said, by way of explanation.

That night, they made camp in a low spot out of the wind. No provisions were supplied the troops, but each man brought his own. Eudora had made a mess of corn pone and put them in a sack for Esker. He shared them with Mosey and Jackson.

"There is nothin' better in this world than a good corn pone," sighed Mosey. "I generally sop mine in molasses, but out here on the baldies, a plain one will do."

They slept on the ground on or under their saddle blankets. Fortunately, there was enough mesquite and cedar in the gullies to keep fires going all night.

CHAPTER 46

Two Bellies and his warriors followed the troops for a day, and when they stopped for the night, the warriors climbed a bluff above the rangers and watched the fires below them. They had never seen such a contingent of armed white men.

"Where are those Texans going?" said Broken Arm. "They look like they want to fight."

"I guess they are going to go kill those Kickapoo," said Two Bellies. "It is important that we know where these Texans are. It is more important that we know where they are not."

Iron Hawk smiled, "I think I would like to get me some more horses."

"And trophies, too," said Broken Arm. "If all of the Texan soldiers are shivering out here on the prairie, we should go see to their women and their houses." He looked at Iron Hawk and smiled, "Their horses too."

The soft ticking of snow on the window pane woke Eudora before dawn. She had a milk cow and a yearling calf to feed before the snow got too deep to pull the barn door open. By the time she got dressed, it was snowing heavily. As she walked to the barn, she listened to the strange quiet the snow always made. It seemed to bury noise as it fell. It had already drifted against the barn door and she struggled with it, cursing Esker's absence. The rattle of gunfire split the silence. Eudora labored through the snow and crested the hill to see where it came from. The nearest house, almost a mile away, was on fire.

She could see riders in its dooryard. Even from that distance, she saw the bright red of blood spilled on the snow.

She rushed inside the house, pulled the rug from the floor, lifted the trap door, and crawled into the root cellar. It was pitch dark and smelled of stale turnips and sprouted potatoes. The only sound was her own breathing. She listened for voices or footsteps, any sound that meant the Indians were in her house. Her fear exhausted her, and eventually she fell asleep. She was awakened by voices and footsteps above her. Suddenly, light spilled into the little cellar, blinding her. The warriors grabbed her hair and pulled her into the room. Each man took his turn. Eudora did not scream, but pulled into herself. She found a place in her mind, a blankness which insulated her from the outrages of the Comanche. She waited to die. When the last man finished, there came a commotion on her outside steps. Iron Hawk laughed and ran to see what had happened. She then heard their horses departing. She lay on the floor, unable to stand or think. She was certain they would return and kill her. But they had left, and Eudora eventually gathered herself and began to wash her body and the floor. She threw her clothes into the fireplace and burned them.

Her house was untouched, though the barn was burned to ashes. The cow and calf had been killed and slaughtered in the yard. That she and her home were left broken but standing was an act of providence, she concluded. Her horse and mule had been taken. She put on her heaviest boots and began the tally of loss in her neighborhood.

"Best way to get through this is to pay mind to someone else's misery," she said to herself. "Best way is to think of it later."

The town itself had been untouched, but several cabins on its outskirts had livestock taken, and when the owners intervened they were killed and their homes burned. The cabin she had seen on fire, she visited first. They were named Johansson, and had three children. Mr. Johansson had left with the rangers, leaving Mrs. Johansson with the children and an aging father. Mrs. Johansson met Eudora on the road to her cabin. Her face was white as a china plate, and she could barely speak. She said the Comanche knocked down the corral and began taking their horses. Her father met the Comanche at the door with a shotgun, and was immediately killed. She took the children into the brush while the Comanche were occupied butchering her father. From the thicket behind her home, she watched it burn to the ground.

Eudora took Mrs. Johansson and her children to her house, and made corn bread and Lincoln coffee, a vile brew made from roasted live oak acorns. Wheat for biscuits was scarce and real coffee was scarcer. She put pallets on the floor for the children, and gave Mrs. Johannson her bed. The next day, she scouted the neighborhood on foot for other victims of the raid. She cursed Captain Price and the rest for leaving the settlement unprotected while they ran off with banners flying. The snow continued to fall through the day. It was still falling the next night. It was the deepest she had ever seen.

Given the deteriorating weather, Two Bellies decided that they should gather the horses and return to the little canyon and wait for the weather to break. Broken Arm was climbing the steps to Eudora's cabin and had slipped on ice and fallen. He had broken his collar bone.

"Maybe we should call you Break Both Arms, now," teased Two Bellies. Broken Arm could only grit his teeth and grin in reply.

They rode into the falling snow, driving their stolen horses before them. The snow had begun to blow up and blizzard. It was getting colder. Broken Arm had taken the elder Johansson's scalp, which had changed from warm and wet to frozen and stiff within minutes of tearing it off the old man's skull. He had tied it to his gear, and it rattled and scraped in the freezing wind.

CHAPTER 47

The sunlight barely penetrated the clouds as it rose the following morning. It made a weak pink smear on the horizon and emitted no warmth. Esker had covered himself with his horse blanket and the heat of his body had turned the snow to ice, gluing him to the ground. Jackson used his knife to chip away at the ice until Esker could wriggle himself free.

"This is not my favorite weather," said Esker. He pulled the bag of Eudora's corn pone from his saddlebag. "I'll be. Even my pone are froze."

He passed around the few he had left. Mosey and Jackson gnawed on them appreciatively. Lieutenant Gibbons rode through camp, his great coat flowing behind him.

"I believe that coat is four times too large for him," observed Mosey. "He could of cut it into blankets and we would of all slept warm."

Esker chewed his pone and talked with his mouth full. "I reckon he was right toasty with his big coat," he said. "I wonder if he sleeps in that pill box of a hat?"

"It would be a handy slop jar, if one had a need out here," said Mosey.

Jackson sat, chewing and looking morose. Esker and Mosey left him alone with his thoughts, which could not be very pleasant ones. He was about to attack his own people, and the whites, the people he had decided to serve, were interested in hanging him. Once he swallowed the last of the pone and swabbed his gums with an index finger, he mounted and rode up to find the Tonkawa scouts.

"I wonder what we are gonna find when we meet up with those Indians, Esker," said Mosey. "We told those Kickapoo just enough to make it easier to kill us."

"Let's keep to the rear, if we can," said Esker. "I want to stay out of this fight if I can. For more reasons than one."

The troops had mounted, formed a column and resumed the trek by the time the sun had cleared the horizon. The snow, which had paused during the night, resumed. The horses and mules struggled through the drifts and the column was strung out for miles. Neither Gibbons nor his horse seemed the least fatigued. He rode up and down the line of men shouting for them to catch up. He gathered the company commanders.

"I just made a head count, and believe we are two dozen fewer than we started with," he said. "You pass the word among your troops that I will execute deserters."

"I suppose some of those missing came up with lame horses, or they froze to death, Lieutenant," said Price. "I can send our scout back to find them."

"No, we can't spare him. We have no use for lame horses, and if the men are not hardy enough for rough travel, we have no need for them either," said Gibbons.

"Some of us ain't as nicely outfitted as you, Lieutenant," said Price. "I'll send one of my troops back to have a look."

Mosey was sent to backtrack the trail. It pleased him to have the wind more or less at his back for a time. After four or five miles, with no track or other sign of the men, he became concerned for his own ability to get back to the column. His horse was already worn. He was about to wheel around and return when he saw six lumps in the snow. He dismounted and approached them. He swept the snow from them and found four dead men and two horses. The men wore light clothing, and the horses were little more than skin and bones.

"Well, that explains four of the two dozen," he thought. He decided they could be buried on the return trip.

Mosey caught up with the column and reported to Price. "I suppose we will find most of the rest of 'em when the snow melts," he said. "Dang, Captain, weren't none of 'em dressed for the weather. What will their mothers think?"

The snow ended though the wind kept much of it in the air for the rest of the day. The scouts could not read the trail for the feet of drifted snow, so they were reliant on Jackson's memory of the surrounding terrain. He knew the course was a little south by west and pushed on. He was unsure of the trail, though he would not show his concern. The column made its camp on high ground that night, exposed to the wind. The swales and creek bottoms were too deep with snow. The sky cleared and the temperature fell so hard that Esker could not feel his feet or his fingers.

"Ain't no one in this troop going to be able to load, let alone pull a trigger by morning," he said.

Mosey dug a little cave into a snow bank and invited Esker in. "This will at least keep the wind off us. We can make a little stick fire, for to keep us for a while."

Jackson sat by a little fire with the Tonkawa scouts. He knew they would reach the Kickapoo the next morning. He was still awake when the first pinks of sunrise began to show.

CHAPTER 48

Despite the recent depredations by the Comanche, the Kickapoo horse guard consisted only of an old man and a gangly boy named Skinny. It was mid-morning, and though the Kickapoo expected the arrival of the Texans, the camp was quiet. Whirlwind was hopeful that if he followed Jackson's suggestion of sending a female messenger with a white flag, that the Texans would be satisfied. Besides, he thought, the weather was bitter, which might deter them for a while. He was enjoying the warmth of his lodge, too. His wife had cut cedar boughs and bark, and with the addition of a few blankets had made a snug wickiup. The snow had drifted against it so that the only evidence that it was there was a thin line of smoke emerging from the hole in its roof.

Jackson saw the smoke of the camp in the little creek valley. It lay among the lodges and trees like a thick bank of fog. Though the snow had ceased, particles of ice shimmered in the air, mixing with the smoke from the camp. He rode back to the troops with difficulty through the deep snow. He crested a hill and saw the column which had become broken clumps of men and horses scattered for several miles. When Jackson informed Gibbons, he halted the column to confer with his company commanders. When they finally assembled, he proclaimed,

"I shall send half the regulars around the left flank to capture the horse herd. The other half I shall send to the right to cut off escape," he said. "Captain Price and the other commanders will hold their troops on this ridge above the

186

camp, and once our regulars are in position, I will fire the howitzer as the signal to advance."

"This camp has all the earmarks of a peaceful bunch, Lieutenant," said Price. "Do you think we should determine their intentions first?"

"Might I assume you have actually been listening to that scout of yours, Captain?" said Gibbons. "Are you a lover of Indians? A squaw man perhaps?" In an open-palmed gesture, he looked around incredulously at the assembled officers. "These noble red pets of yours, Captain, are nothing but lice ridden vermin." He turned toward the huge horse herd below them and pulled on his little beard. "Besides, the Cause has need of a great deal of horse flesh, and that camp is our commissary." He walked away, chuckling.

It took until noon for Gibbons to place his troops. A few Kickapoo, wrapped in blankets, came out into the weather to watch. Whirlwind was among them. He sent a young woman, a cousin named Pierced Nose, to carry the white flag and the message of their peaceful intentions. She was pregnant and slow negotiating the climb up the ridge, where Gibbons and his howitzer waited. Gibbons laughed to himself at the spectacle of her waddling stiff-legged up the hill, burdened by her swollen belly and a bed sheet attached to a stick.

She smiled, breathless from the exertion, and said in perfect English, "Lieutenant, we are Kickapoo, and have no reason for trouble here. We will leave in the morning and will keep traveling till we reach Mexico." Gibbons was silent, his face drawn into a scowl. Pierced Nose thought perhaps she had been unclear. "We are peaceful, Lieutenant. We don't want to fight nobody. If you talk to our chief, I think you will understand."

Gibbons drew his revolver and pointed it at her head. "I recognize no peaceful Indians in Texas." He pulled the trigger and a pink spray of blood and matter stained the snow. He ordered the howitzer to fire, the signal to attack.

The company officers were stunned. "You goddamned son-of-a-bitch," hissed Price, who tried to grab his pistol. Gibbons pointed it at him.

"If you disobey my order, I will shoot you where you stand," he sneered. "We are engaged in battle. There's no turning back, now, and I will not brook further insubordination. Especially from you."

Jackson had led the regulars to their position near the horse herd. They dismounted and hid behind a low terrace downstream from the camp. He heard the pistol shot and turned in time to see the woman drop the white flag and fall. The troopers around him turned as well.

"Well ain't he a little Bantam rooster today?" said the sergeant in charge of the left flank. The thud of the howitzer rolled across the valley. The sergeant turned to his men, grinning. "Guess the party is on! Let's get them horses, boys!!"

The troopers mounted and then charged the horse herd, which scattered in every direction. There were more than five hundred horses. Gibbons watched through his field glass from his vantage point but the horses kicked up so much snow they were almost invisible. The boy, Skinny, and the old man who were guarding them dropped their rifles and stood, amazed.

Two soldiers captured them without resistance and with their rifles pointed at their backs, marched them toward Gibbons' command. The old man fell every few steps, and one trooper dismounted and carried him most of the way. The rest of the troops scattered to gather the horses.

"We have prisoners for you, Lieutenant!" yelled the one trooper still on horseback. It was his first skirmish, and he felt proud that he had accomplished some little thing. He cast his eye around to see if anyone had taken notice.

"We are not taking prisoners today, Private," said Gibbons. "Shoot them."

"Hell, Lieutenant," said the soldier who had carried the old man up the snowy slope. "This is just an old man and a boy. They did not even put up a fight, but surrendered right away."

Gibbons unholstered his pistol and shot the old man in his wrinkled forehead. "Now shoot that boy!"

"Nawsir. I got God to answer to more than you, Lieutenant. I'll get hell fire if I kill a child."

"You have disobeyed a direct order, trooper, and shall suffer the consequences," said Gibbons. He shot the boy, who fell and rolled a few yards down the slope, his long arms and legs flailing through the snow.

Price ordered his company forward and on foot, and they stumbled through snow drifts down the ridge toward the camp. They were in the open and exposed to the scattered fire which came from the creek bank below them. Esker saw plumes of smoke from each rifle shot as well as the steaming breath rising from the shooters. The troopers whooped and grinned as they charged down the slope, pausing to shoot and kicking up spumes of snow as they ran. The Kickapoo rose from cover and fired a volley which brought down the first ranks. Esker thought it looked like some invisible force had just swung a scythe through them. The ardor of the following ranks evaporated quickly. The advance halted and all but a few fell on their bellies in the snow and returned fire. The few who tried to resume the advance were soon felled.

Esker saw Mosey a few yards behind him. "I thought we were gonna stick to the rear of this mess!" he yelled to Mosey, who grimaced and crawled forward to join him.

"Well, the dang last rank is now the front rank," he hissed. "We are goin' ta be hunkered down here till nightfall, unless them gray boys on the right flank relieve us," he said.

On the right flank, Sergeant McCourtey was proud of the command Gibbons had given him. He spread his forty regulars in the brush upstream from the camp. They had occupied the position for almost an hour when the howitzer fired. As expected, the Kickapoo women and children attempted to flee upstream, and they had sent them scurrying with a single rifle volley. Though a few were killed, the thick brush had absorbed most of the fire. In the distance, they heard the rifle fire of the advancing minutemen and volunteers, but their view was obscured by the brush. They crouched among the little trees along the creek and listened to the battle.

"I suspect most of that rifle fire is them Injuns in this here very creekbed," McCourtey said to his troops scattered in the brush. He cocked an ear. The fire from the troops was scattered with long pauses between shots. "Sounds like those boys are takin' a lickin'." He had been ordered to hold his position and prevent the Indians' escape, but the lure of glory was too much. He stood and addressed his troops in a loud voice. "Boys, I tell you what we'll do. We are going to advance down this creek to draw the Injuns into a fight, and relieve them fellers pinned down on the ridge."

He stood, raised his saber and waved his troops forward. When he turned to lead the charge, he was knocked to the ground by a bullet in his shoulder. He regained his feet and saw more than fifty of the Kickapoo advancing on his right flank. Though the wind was knocked out of him, he commanded his troops to return fire on the right.

Whirlwind spread his warriors out into a skirmish line along a stand of cedar trees uphill from the Texans. He saw they had perfect ground to thin their ranks one by one. McCourty quickly recognized his position was untenable.

"First rank, on my signal run like hell up this creek!! Second rank keep shootin' till I tell you to run."

When the first rank began to scatter, Whirlwind saw their chance to over-run their position. They descended on the fleeing soldiers, howling. A few soldiers knelt behind cover and tried to repel the charge, while the remainder dropped their rifles and scattered. The few who remained were reloading their muskets when the warriors swamped them. The warriors too, had empty rifles but they killed the soldiers with their knives and rifle butts. They chased the remainder, who were trying to make the ridge, bludgeoning those who fell behind.

Blood stained the cold water which flowed back to McCourty's position. He expected the Indians to immediately attack from upstream, and spread his men across it like a dam. Several of them stood in the icy, bloody water and waited, shivering with the cold and fear. There was no sound other than the rush of water over the rocks. The sun was low in the west burning red against the low clouds. A strange feeling of peace, of rest, mocked them. McCourty was disturbed at the silence and looked about, fearing the attack would come from a direction other than he expected. His force was decimated by half. He would try to hold his position, but expected a slaughter.

The attack came below them. Whirlwind's warriors descended on the remnant, and killed or wounded every man. Sergeant McCourtey sat down in the freezing water, and waited for his turn to die. He passively watched his troopers being hacked to death in the stream until finally, an arrow found his heart.

The volunteers had lain listening to the fight developing along the little creek to their right. It had apparently pulled some of the Indians from their front and the firing lessened.

"Esker, I reckon this may be as good as it gets. Let's shimmy back over the ridge," said Mosey, who was already turning on his belly to make the long crawl.

"You think Gibbons will shoot us for bein' cowards?" said Esker.

"I think I would rather take that chance than stay," said Mosey, who had already gotten a few yards ahead.

The rest of the volunteers had begun to retreat. Some ran and some crawled back to the top of the ridge where Gibbons and most of the volunteer company commanders waited. Gibbons' face was red with fury, and his little chin beard trembled.

"Cowards!!" he screamed shrilly, and brandished his pistol. He turned to Price and the other commanders. "Turn these men around!! Attack!! Attack!!" He turned his pistol on Price.

"I told you I would shoot you on sight if you disobeyed my orders," he said. "Rally your men or I will kill you where you stand."

Down slope the Kickapoo had regrouped, and fired on the retreating troops. A few within range of the Indians dropped as they ran through the snow, but most had reached a safe distance.

"Lieutenant," said Price calmly. "We are out-gunned, out-manned, and we have what amounts to an entrenched enemy. I will not send my men down there to be slaughtered."

Jackson stood a few feet behind Price, listening impassively. He had seen the Kickapoo woman murdered. He had been told of the murder of the old man and boy. He would not let Gibbons murder Captain Price.

Gibbons cocked his pistol and shoved the barrel into Price's chest. "Do your duty, Captain, or die." He had inhaled to begin another tirade when Jackson passed his knife neatly around Gibbons' throat, releasing a torrent of blood which immediately soaked his immaculate uniform. Later, it seemed strange to Jackson that his only thought at the time was how unhappy Gibbons would feel at being so soiled. Gibbons' knees buckled and he fell to the ground, staining the trampled snow. Jackson knelt and unhooked the strap which held Gibbons little pill box on his head. He pulled it off and scalped him. He would present the scalp as a gift to Whirlwind, a gesture of apology, of reconciliation.

Price and the other commanders stood dumbstruck. As Jackson worked on Gibbons' corpse, Price bent down and rested a hand on his shoulder.

"That will do Jackson. That is sufficient." He pulled him away and led him to his horse. Jackson held the dripping scalp by its long greasy hair, leaving a trail of blood across the snow.

"You must leave now," said Price. Though I will not argue the right of what you did, the law will." He looked away from Jackson for a moment, silent. He sucked his teeth and turned back to him. "An Indian don't have any standin' under the law. By all rights I should arrest you, but since you have done the only justice performed here today, I am going to give you a head start." He stepped away from Jackson's horse. "I wish you hadn't scalped him, though."

Jackson said nothing. He kicked his horse and headed southwest and toward the hardest of the hard country.

CHAPTER 49

"Where is Jackson?" said Esker. "Did he make it?"

Price pointed to Gibbons' bloody corpse. "We will not see him for some time to come, I'd conjecture," he said.

Esker knelt and ran his gloved fingers over the former site of the Lieutenant's scalp.

"My lord," he whispered. "My lord, he scalped him."

"Cut his throat, too. Well, I suppose he intended to offer up the scalp to his friends as compensation for what they will view as his treachery. I doubt they will think too favorably of him after all this," said Price.

The Kickapoo ceased fire as soon as the Texans had made it clear they were in full retreat. Horses and men had already begun straggling back to the northeast in a broken column, riders and men on foot struggling alike through the deep snow. Captain Price gathered what remained of his company, and pulled them into a column.

"I fear more of us are going to succumb to the weather than what was killed by the Indians," said Mosey. "When that sun gets good and down, it is going to get good and cold."

Price knew it as a fact. He knew if they did not find shelter somewhere, the wounded would probably die, and not a few of those unscathed in battle. He remembered a dugout and a few outbuildings less than five miles north of the trail. He had encountered it on a scout, years before. The man lived alone, and was not friendly. Price suspected that he had long ago fled some malfeasance in the settlements and had hid himself underground beyond the frontier. He suspected that the old man eventually forgot why he was hiding. He seemed addled, in addition to seeming a little mean.

Price pushed his horse through the snow to catch up with the remaining regulars. "Who is in command?" Price hollered at the slumped backs of the retreating soldiers.

A single man turned to him. He was bearded and icicles hung from his face. "We got a corporal, left, I guess." He pointed to a rider near the head of the column.

"Corporal!" shouted Price as he rode up. "It is going to get dark soon, and we need to get out of the weather. These men are going to freeze. Especially the wounded." He described the location of the dugout. "I recommend we try to make it there. We can take shelter in shifts, and though I don't expect it to be comfortable, we might all survive."

"We are going to press on, Captain," said the corporal, who had only accidentally been promoted, and wished he had only himself to look out for. "If these men stop moving, they are going to freeze. We're going to press for the settlements."

"It took us almost three days to make the trip out, Corporal. We were all mounted, and the snow not as deep. Those men on foot won't make it more than a day," said Price. "I don't suppose we ended up with any of those Indian horses?" said Price.

"No, we did not. They were headed south and were in much better shape than those chasin' them. I wish we had those and a few to eat as well, but we don't," said the corporal, who was tiring of the conversation.

"Well, sir, I suppose I will take my company to shelter, and wish you the best of luck, Corporal," said Price, extending his hand.

"Suit yourself," said the corporal, keeping his free hand tucked under his arm for the warmth.

Within a few hours, the search for the dugout began to appear to be a mistake. The sky began clearing showing scattered stars, the temperature fell, and the wind began kicking up a blizzard. Esker could not raise his face into the wind for fear of a frostbitten nose. All the men kept their heads down, their chins resting on their chests. He feared the horses' eyelids would freeze and they would go blind. However, their mounts kept the same heading with determination, perhaps smelling strange horses or feed at the dugout.

Either by equine sense of smell, or divine intervention, thought Price, they made the dugout intact and without a loss of man or horse by midnight. It was a miracle too, that they found it at all, since the snow had it blanketed, making it just another bump in a bumpy landscape. Only a stove pipe emitting a tendril of smoke marked it. Fortunately, a horse stall and a smokehouse stood far enough above the snow to make the place detectable.

Esker dismounted, climbed the mound of snow, and shouted down the stove pipe. "We are rangers in need of shelter!!" He waited a moment for an answer. He tapped on the stove pipe with the barrel of his pistol. "Open up!! We are the Price Company of the 2nd division Frontier Organization, and we demand you open up!"

A voice came up the pipe. "I don't keer. Go away!"

"Goddamnit! Open up or we will dig you out!!" shouted Esker, exasperated.

"I ain't skeert. Go away!" said the voice.

"He's holed up like a possum, Captain," said Mosey.

Price dismounted and took his bedroll from his saddle. He climbed the snowy mound and stuffed the wadded blanket down the stovepipe. He and Esker stood listening with their ears pressed against its top. First, they heard a muffled shout, then coughing and then retching.

"Get the dang snow off the door, damnit, I cain't open it!!" the voice shouted up the chimney.

After digging a few minutes, the rangers exposed a door which was instantly shoved open from inside. A billow of smoke and a dirty, skinny old man rolled out. When he finished coughing and spitting, he looked at the forty rangers gathered at his door.

"Well, hell, cain't all of you sons-a-bitches fit in there!!" he said.

"We will go in groups of five. Every man will get thirty minutes. The others can wait in the horse stall or the smokehouse. Get a fire goin' in there if you can," said Price to the men. "You can stay in the dugout, and we'll try not to discommode you more than is necessary," he said to the old man, who had retreated back to the fire.

They situated their wounded in the warmth first. Others looked for a woodpile or anything that would burn. The woodpile could not be located, and after further searching Esker determined they would dismantle the horse shed and build a bonfire. He was sure Price would find some way to compensate the man, but in either case, it did not weigh on his conscience. Though the wounded men were allowed to languish in the heat, each man was given a few turns in the dugout.

The sun came up clear. Though still bitterly cold, the sun held some heat. By the time the troops were mounted and in motion again, the snow had begun to melt. By the time they came to the hills west of Hamerton, most of the men wearing coats had shed them.

"Don't that beat all?" said Mosey to Esker. "We were dang near at the North Pole froze to death last night, and now it's like spring in Tennessee."

Esker smiled at him. "I'll take a Tennessee spring any day," he said, though he had never been there. Mosey had grown up in Tennessee, and according to him, it was the seat of the most temperate of weather.

A sorrowful thought struck Mosey, and his face reflected it. "When this snow melts off, we will have to go collect our boys who didn't make it. Or bury what we find of them where they lay."

On the third day, they crested a rise west of Hamerton, and the whole of the settlement lay before them. Esker grinned. His heart leapt at the thought of seeing Eudora and sleeping warm in her smokehouse again. He saw her dog run on the edge of town, and then saw the burned cabins nearby.

"Oh my lord," said Esker. "The Comanches have tried to raze the town."

CHAPTER 50

It was dusk before Esker walked into Eudora's cabin. It had taken most of the day to tend to equipment and horses. Price had given all but five rangers leave to check on their families and livestock.

Esker opened Eudora's door cautiously. He had been told by the wife of one of the rangers that Eudora had been outraged by the Comanche and he feared she might be sensitive to sudden noises. He found Mrs. Johansson sitting by the fire with her girls. His heart sank. He had seen her husband fall in the first minutes of the battle with the Kickapoo. He knew he would be the one to tell her.

"Mrs. Johansson? I am Esker Doyle, Eudora's man." He blushed at the unintended insinuation, so he rephrased. "Well, I meant to say, I am her help, I suppose. Is she here?"

Mrs. Johansson did not smile. "She is in the barn, trying to get a borrowed milch cow to squirt." She looked at Esker accusingly. "They kilt her cow and her cow's calf, you know. They burnt my house and kilt my father. They did other things, too, while you and Mr. Johansson was a'gallopin' about." She craned her neck to peer out the open door. "Where is my husband? Did he not follow you here?"

Esker pulled a chair close to Mrs. Johansson, and sagged into it. "Ma'am? I have most distressing news for you." He reached for her hand, but she drew it away. The little girl sitting in her lap stared at him without expression. "It pains me more than I can say to tell you that your husband was killed by the Indians."

She looked at him blankly, then adjusted her seat. "Well, it surprises me none. The good Lord has seen fit to take most ever-thing I have." She put her hand over the crown of her daughter's head as though to keep her from floating away. "If it pleases God, I would prefer that He leave me my children." She stood the little girl on her feet and walked her into the adjoining room. She turned back to Esker. "Where is his corpse? I should like to see him buried proper."

Esker's mouth went dry. "We left him on the battlefield, Ma'am. Our retreat was a hasty one, and we hardly had time to gather the wounded, let alone the dead. Captain Price will send the Company back to collect him shortly, I am sure."

"Captain Price will? Will he?" she said coldly. "I hate to think that the varmints will be at him." She turned again to walk through the door. "But they will. And there won't be much for you to bring back to me." A sob caught her, and she fled the room.

Esker found Eudora in the barn. She sat disheveled, on a milking stool, working the cow's teats vigorously. A lantern lit her back and her auburn hair stood out like a halo. Esker had never seen someone as angelic. His breath caught in his throat, and he struggled to speak.

"Eudora?" he said, almost a whisper.

"I heard you ride up," she said, without looking up. "I suppose you boys noticed things were not as you left them."

202

"Yes, ma'am," said Esker. He did not know how to ask her. "Are you well?"

She turned to him. The lantern illuminated her bruised face. "Goddamnit no, Esker! I am in no way well!" She began to weep. Esker sat beside her and absently patted her knee.

"It will pass, Eudora. With God's help, your wounds of body and spirit will heal. You must give it time. Time is all it will take," said Esker.

She slapped his face with the full force of her open palm. "Damn you, and all of you for leaving this town defenseless!" she hissed. "And you have no idea how deep this hurt lies. I am ruined!! Ruined!! Do you understand?!" she sobbed. "I've but no doubt my husband will abandon me for being soiled by the Indians."

"It would take a heartless man to do that," said Esker, softly. He knew it was common for marriages to dissolve when the wife was outraged by Indians, but he couldn't think of anything more comforting. "If you were my wife, I would not abandon you, Eudora," he said. "I love you." She stared at him as though he had passed gas in her presence.

"You are a child, Esker!! Just a snot-nosed boy, and how dare you say such ridiculous things." She picked up her milking stool and lantern and brushed Esker out of the way.

CHAPTER 51

Two Bellies tried to untie the knot on the horse's hackamore. It had loosened on the ride back from the settlement, and now the cold and damp made the rawhide too stiff to work, and made his fingers stiff and sore as well.

"You should have brought your wife with you," said Iron Hawk. "Women are better at tying things." It was a sincere observation, but Two Bellies heard criticism. He cut the rope and began retying it.

"Yes. I have a young wife. Not like yours who is old and smells bad," Two Bellies replied. "The snow is melting. If we ride while the ground is still frozen, it will not show our tracks. You need to prepare," he said. "You do want some of these horses, do you not?"

Iron Hawk knew Two Bellies was in a bad mood. It seemed each time he spoke to him, he made Two Bellies mad somehow. He decided to talk to Broken Arm instead. Broken Arm's shoulder hurt, and he was in a bad mood, too.

"Why do you always tell me Two Bellies is in a bad mood?" he said, exasperated. "I don't care what kind of mood he is in. I have a pain in my arm."

Iron Hawk walked out to talk to the horses and to catch his own. The three young warriors were guarding the herd, and though he thought of talking to them, they would have nothing to say about the nature of Two Bellies' dark moods. The sun was almost overhead by the time they began to move the herd north. It shown so bright on the melting snow that Broken

Arm had to shield his eyes against it. Despite his pain, he was excited by the horses and goods they had taken from the Texans. The herd, numbering more than thirty, stretched before them impressively. Many of them were poor, but the winter would be long, and those horses would feed the camp for weeks. He had taken a scalp, too, from an old man who hadn't had much hair on the crown of his head, so he scalped him from the nape of his neck to the edge of his bald pate. He had also taken a knife and a shotgun. He would be proud when he rode into the camp.

The snow melted quickly, and the ground turned to mud. Their trail would be obvious to any observer, thought Two Bellies, who suggested they should camp for a few days until it dried, but Iron Hawk disagreed.

"Those Texans are too busy wasting their time on scared women and the dead men they left on the creek to follow us. I think we should go home."

Two Bellies grunted and pointed his horse to a knoll topped by a thick cedar brake. He would camp there, and it was big enough to hold their stolen horses, for a little while, at least. The cedar would hide them, but the winter grasses were thin, and the forage poor. He enjoyed the warming sun, which rose with greater intensity each day that the wind blew from the south. Despite Iron Hawk's objections, they stayed in camp for three days, and Two Bellies smoked and let the rising sun warm his face. His body ached sometime. He knew he was not the warrior he had once been. When he was young, women watched him from the corner of their eyes, and smiled shyly at him. Now that he was getting old, his gaze was not reciprocated. He had outlived two wives. The sister of the younger of the two, Grasshopper, had come to live with him and be his wife after her husband was killed by the Utes. She was young and her skin was soft. He liked to lay with her, but he liked the way she cared for him more. She rubbed his sore legs and back. She brushed and braided his hair and worked hard like a woman should. He missed her. He was ready to go home.

The snow melted and the ground dried, leaving all the grasses the same color. They had been all hues of red and brown before the snow, but now they were bleached. The prairie rolled before them in shades of tan and white, which always reminded Iron Hawk that winter had truly arrived.

"Do you remember seeing buffalo in this part of the plain?" said Iron Hawk to Two Bellies.

"Yes," he replied. "They used to be so thick here that it would take a day to ride across the herd." He smiled. "When I was young, our hunts were far south of here. This was the country of the Nokoni, and it would have been bad manners to take their buffalo. But, maybe we did sometime. A little."

Iron Hawk smiled. "It is good that we have horses to eat. I would like it better if we had buffalo. Maybe we will see some before we get back to camp."

Two Bellies smiled at Iron Hawk. It made Iron Hawk feel a little better. Maybe talking about the old days was a way to get on better with him, he thought.

The good weather held until the last two days of the trip. The band had moved camp to the valley of the Cimarron, where there were cottonwood trees for fires and cottonwood bark for the ponies to eat. The storm approached them from the northwest, and it started with wind, rain and lightning. After a few hours of hail and pelting rain, sleet began to fall, and they had difficulty facing the herd into the gale. Though Iron Hawk and Broken Arm wore wool blankets over their shirts, Two Bellies was wrapped in a buffalo robe.

"Why don't you give me your robe for a little while," said Broken Arm. "This cold makes my arm hurt more."

"Next time we kill buffalo, you should get your wife to make you one," said Two Bellies, teasing, because he knew Broken Arm was unmarried.

"I do not have a wife," said Broken Arm. "You should give me the robe as a present for when I do marry."

"No," said Two Bellies. "But now that you have horses, you will find a woman who might marry even you."

Broken Arm did not appreciate Two Bellies' humor. His blanket was full of water from the rain, and now it stiffened with frost. He was thinking of shooting and skinning a horse for its hide to wear when the river valley and the camp appeared. He kicked his horse and whooped, charging the village, and driving the horses ahead of him. Iron Hawk laughed and signaled to the young warriors to follow. Two Bellies scanned the river valley in search of his lodge. He found it, standing near the river. It was large, and though unadorned with paint, it was bright and new. Grasshopper had sewn a new cover the winter before. However, no smoke rose from its smoke hole.

He tied his horse next to the lodge and entered. It was dark. There had been no fire at its hearth for some time, and Grasshopper's robes and clothing were gone. His mind raced. "Had she been killed?" he wondered. "Had she been kidnapped?" He rushed to the lodge of his friend, White Man Likes Him, who was too old to hunt or raid and spent most of his time meddling in other people's affairs. Two Bellies scratched at the lodge door, and was invited in. White Man was lying on his robes while his wife, at least as old as he, cooked on the fire at the center of the lodge. White Man sat up and smiled at Two Bellies.

"I am happy to see you. Do you want to eat?"

"I am looking for my wife. She is gone from my lodge," said Two Bellies, foregoing politeness, since his visit was urgent, and White Man could drag visits on for hours.

White Man stroked his chin, and made a croaking sound at the back of his throat.

"It is an unfortunate thing, I think. I think maybe Hair Rope decided to make her his wife. I think maybe she decided that way too."

Two Bellies tossed the door flap aside and strode to his horse. He pulled his pistol from a fringed leather bag he kept tied to his saddle. Hair Rope's lodge was easy to find. He had a dozen fine horses picketed behind it. He threw open the lodge door, and caught Grasshopper by her hair. In an instant, he cut off her nose before Hair Rope had risen from his bed.

"Brother!" he pleaded. "I will give you five of the horses picketed behind my lodge. You can pick the ones you want."

As he spoke, he pulled his own knife and held it behind his back.

Two Bellies did not speak, but advanced on Hair Rope who, due to the smallness of his lodge, had no place to retreat. Two Bellies slashed at Hair Rope, ripping his belly. He fired his pistol grazing Hair Rope's temple. Hair Rope instantly lunged and buried his knife to its hilt in Two Bellies' chest. Two Bellies sat down, looking at the handle of the knife protruding from his ribs. It rose and fell with each heartbeat. He looked longingly at Grasshopper, who was trying to stanch the copious flow of blood from her bobbed nose. He looked at Hair Rope, shook his head, and muttering complaints, lay down on the cold earth of the lodge floor, and died.

Hair Rope and Grasshopper gathered a few possessions, and after packing the lodge, they left the camp. The people stood watching them go, but no one interfered. Both were bleeding badly, and were a little unsteady from the loss of blood. Hair Rope knew a camp of the Kiowa where they could stay.

"The Kiowa people are never surprised by what our people do," he said teasingly to Grasshopper. I think if we stay away for a couple of winters, our people will have forgotten. I don't like what your old husband did to your nose, though. Maybe you should stay with the Kiowa until a new one grows back."

CHAPTER 52

Andrew Jackson had ridden a long way southwest. So far that there were tall yuccas instead of trees, and wide gaps between clumps of grass. He had ridden out of the snow days before, and now he camped on a little butte, overlooking part of the old Comanche trail which ran from the plains into Mexico. He waited for the Kickapoo. He did not sleep, and though his mind held much scripture, none of it comforted him. He decided that his soul had left him.

The Kickapoo arrived two days later, and had taken almost an hour to pass below him. It was clear that they had left most of their belongings behind. Most were on foot, since their horses had been scattered. At the end of the long line, two mules dragged the Howitzer and caisson the Texans had left behind. They looked poor and ragged. He followed the band for some time, lagging behind the rear guard, hoping to be seen. Eventually, Whirlwind rode back and stopped him.

"Why are you here?" he said flatly. "You are an enemy now."

"I brought you the Lieutenant's scalp," said Jackson. He had tied the scalp to a long yucca stalk like a banner. "I took his scalp, and I am giving it to you now."

Whirlwind took the scalp and examined it. He looked at Jackson, his eyes narrowed. "You are not a Kickapoo," he spat. "I do not think you ever were. You are not even a good imitation of a white man. You are a misshapen creature of some unknown kind." He shoved the scalp at Jackson. "You leave now before you infect us."

"Maybe you should kill me," said Jackson.

"I will not do you that honor," said Whirlwind.

Jackson sat on the little butte, and watched the people disappear on the horizon. He absently stroked Gibbons' scalp like one might stroke a cat. Jackson knew that Whirlwind was truthful. He had failed in all things. He had betrayed his people, and had murdered his white commander. He was neither white nor Kickapoo, and now he was despised by both. He let his horse go. He had decided to die.

The winter sun was not intense, but the air and the land were dry. By the end of the fourth day without water, his tongue swelled and filled his mouth. He could not swallow. He decided to look for a drink. The Pecos was not so far away, but when he tried to stand, his legs would not support him. It amused him a little, that he had decided to live only to discover his body would not let him. It had made its decision, and he trusted it. He lay down on the rocky ground as night crept in. Though the air was cold, the rock still held some warmth, and it seeped into his body. The stars were his witnesses. They stood vigil. He mused that they were the souls of those who had crossed over long ago — the old ones who saw a different land in different times and knew different sorrows.

When the sun set on the sixth day, Jackson was no longer thirsty. He could no longer move, but he was at peace. Deep in the night, a dark cloud moved across the sky. Fat drops fell, and distant thunder muttered. The storm moved over the little butte, and in the flash of lightning, Jackson saw the scattered grasses and the wet ground. He felt glad for the growing things. He felt the earth open its maw for a deep drink. He felt the earth open its maw to swallow him. He closed his eyes.

CHAPTER 53

Esker had never seen such dry country. The dust was so thick on his clothes, they felt stiff and heavy. The troop had been riding south for days, and rivers were becoming scarce. They camped on the Pecos and watered the horses, but a few of the men refused to drink the water. It tasted bad, they said, and they believed it to be so alkaline that it would upset their digestion.

"I'd rather have the shits than die of thirst," said Mosey after draining his canteen. "It don't taste particularly appetizin', but it will do."

Esker drank as much as he could stand, but his stomach began to cramp shortly after. He looked about anxiously. "I hate to take my ease out here in the open," he said. "It makes me appreciate having a bush or two ready nearby."

"Well ain't we delicate," said Mosey. "I should have brought along a bead curtain and a chamber pot to accommodate your sensitivity."

Captain Price sat on a rock and cleaned his pistols. He had been particularly quiet since they had left the settlement. He had tried to refuse the mission, but Major Erath had declined to let the burden of capturing Price's scout fall to another. It was well known that he had allowed Jackson's escape, and to those who had not witnessed Gibbons' behavior, he had done the unthinkable if not the treasonous. Gibbons was not popular, but he was an officer of the Confederacy. Certain things were due him, Erath had said.

Price had rightly assumed that Jackson would follow the Kickapoo south into Mexico. Their trail was obvious. He did not rush, though. Price hoped Jackson would make it south of the Rio Bravo, so he could be done with the affair. Jackson had been a reliable scout, and had never given him trouble.

"I hate to think we should have to shoot Jackson," said Esker who had just returned from what little brush he could find.

"Well. If he don't put up a fight, and we arrest him, his hangin' is a certainty," said Mosey. "If it were me, I would prefer a bullet to a rope."

"Maybe we won't find him," said Esker. "Or maybe the Kickapoo have taken him in, and won't let us take him."

"Ye Gods, Esker! Those Kickapoo are still mad at us. If we see that bunch, we will do well to turn about and run home."

A day beyond the Pecos, one of the rangers pointed to turkey vultures hovering over a little butte west of the trail. The troop found Jackson's remains at its top. The vultures grudgingly moved away from the corpse and, given the opportunity, instantly crow-hopped back. Half of the troop managed the buzzards while the rest stacked rocks over what had been Jackson, and then gathered his weapons. Esker had dreaded a confrontation with Jackson, but had never imagined finding him dead. He picked up the Sharp's rifle they had taken from Orvis Peck.

"You should keep that," said Captain Price. "I know he carried it when the two of you arrived in Hamerton."

"Yes. I killed a man and took it from him," Esker said. "Only fitting that it should haunt me, I guess."

"Well, I suppose this simplifies the matter," said Price. "I despise the idea of burying a man of value, let alone one of our own." He looked around at the men, who held their hats in their hands. "But the idea of shootin' or hangin' the man would have been more than I could stand."

"What do you suppose killed him, Captain?" asked a skinny young ranger who had recently joined the troop. "Both his guns is loaded, so he wasn't in a skirmish."

"No arrows or a sign of a gunshot wound on him that I could see," said Mosey. "Though there warn't much of him left to inspect, I suppose. You don't think he did himself, do ye?"

"Don't talk that way. It was snakebite. A snakebite was what it was," said Esker. "Andrew Jackson was my friend, and he pulled me out of more scrapes than I can count. He was a good man, and there ain't a man in this troop who would say otherwise." He blotted tears on his muddy cheek with the heel of his hand. "I will miss him badly." He walked down the slope to finish crying in private.

CHAPTER 54

Eudora knew she was pregnant long before Dr. Fuhlendorf confirmed it. It was a bitter irony. She and Albert Sydney had prayed for a child; had had for a while, relations so frequently it had been indecent. Three men had raped her. Five minutes and three nasty little squirts later she was with child. She did not even know which man was the father.

She spared Albert Sydney the news for a month after she knew. Finally, she mailed the letter she had written the day Fuhlendorf had confirmed her pregnancy. Each day, she went to Captain Price's store where mail was delivered, hoping for, but dreading his reply. This possibility had, of course, never been discussed, though she knew his sentiments about such exigencies from prior comments. On the occasion of the return of a female captive who had been adopted by the Comanche, and from whom she had returned pregnant, Albert Sydney had insisted that smothering her with a pillow would have been an act of kindness. The girl and her baby had instead died in childbirth- a far more acceptable outcome for the family and community than her having borne a brown-skinned, raven-haired pup.

Mrs. Johansson continued living with her girls at Eudora's cabin. She ate Eudora's food and continued to occupy her bed. She spoke little and she never mentioned Eudora's swelling belly, though she looked at her with such a dour expression that Eudora wanted to slap her. She resisted the impulse, though and spent more time in town to avoid her company. Finally, Mrs. Johansson addressed the matter.

"It is the Lord's retribution," she said.

"What?" said Eudora. "Retribution for what!?"

"You carryin' that spawn of the devil," she said smugly. "My pastor says that your un-churchliness, and high opinion of yourself has led to your downfall." Gleeful hate gleamed in her little black eyes. "I too, have witnessed your blasphemy when you harshly spake to your milch cow," she sneered. "The Lord hath spewed you out of his mouth!"

By nightfall, Eudora had moved all of Mrs. Johansson's belongings to the dooryard. She suggested that she contact a neighboring relative to collect her and her daughters. She packed them a picnic and sent them on their way. She watched the little queue snake its way down the hill toward town. Esker too, watched them wind their way. The sun was setting, and all of them wore the black of mourning. They looked like a little flock of ravens. He was glad to see them go. Though Mrs. Johansson ignored him, one of the little girls had been particularly mean to him, putting grass burs in his blankets and teasing him that his smoke house smell made her sick to her stomach.

He sometimes walked to Price's store with Eudora, and though she tolerated his company, she said little to him. Her anxiety had taken her appetite, and though her belly continued to grow, she had become pale and thin.

"It concerns me that you do not eat enough, Eudora," Esker said one morning as he ate her corn bread and drank her chicory coffee.

"What I eat is of no concern to you, Esker," she said, and slammed a stove lid into place so hard the others jumped out of their seats.

Esker shifted uncomfortably in his chair and said, "Eudora, I am a true friend, despite what you think of me. Unless you turn me out, I will be here to help you after this child is born. I won't leave you. I'm gonna stand up for you where the others will persecute you." He rose from his chair, and stood looking into Eudora's face. He thought her expression had softened, a little. He reached for her hand and said, "But you must accept my concern, Eudora. You must let yourself be my concern. You may not feel the affection I feel for you, but please accept mine as honest, if nothin' else. Consider it a gift, without anticipation of return."

She smiled up at him. A tear slid down her cheek. "Well, ain't we eloquent, this mornin', Mr. Doyle."

The following afternoon, Eudora returned with a letter from Albert Sydney. Her face was ashen, and the letter unopened. She found Esker behind the cabin, planting the vegetable garden. It was now early spring; the prairie began to show its first flowers, and it was warm enough for Esker to break a sweat. He wiped his brow and turned and smiled at Eudora, but his face fell when he saw hers.

"My lord. What is it, Eudora?"

She held the letter out to Esker, and taking it from her hand saw it was from her husband.

"Read it to me," she said. "I don't think I can bear it."

Esker fetched the milking stool for her and seated himself on the ground before her. He pulled the letter from the envelope. It was a single sheet of rough paper, and it rustled in the wind as he unfolded it.

Esker began,

Eudora,

I am in receipt of your letter. It is with great consternation that I read of your misfortune. However, it is with no small irritation that I remind you that I directed you to move to town against this very eventuality. This has been precipitated by your disobedience to your husband's will, and you have reap't what you have sown.

I now direct you to return to Edgefield County, S.C., where you will stay under the care of your mother's family. Though the war has been hard there, I am hopeful that there will be someone to receive you. You may take what little remains of our funds for your travel and support. You must begin this journey as soon as it can be arranged.

If you deliver this child alive, it shall be placed with a convent where it shall remain. In no event shall it bear or be referred to by my family's name. You shall henceforth have no contact with it. I determine that you shall remain with your people in South Carolina, there being no further need for you to return to Texas.

Your Obd't Srvt,
Albert Sydney Carson

Esker folded the letter and returned it to the envelope. He turned his eyes to Eudora, who had sat silently through the reading. He did not expect the face he saw. It was red with anger, and the muscles of her jaw stood out.

"That damnable little man," she hissed. "We shall see who leaves Texas." She immediately returned to the cabin, sat at the kitchen table and wrote:

Albert Sydney,

It is with great consternation that I read of your thin commitment to your vows of marriage. I intend to have this child. I will not do him the dishonor of giving him your name, but he will bear my own. I shall not only stay in Texas, but will continue to occupy the cabin where my child shall be raised. As concerns the offer of funds for our support, I gladly accept.

As it is evident that your small virtues of charity and love toward me would go a long way toward freezing beer, I suggest that there is no further need for you to return to your former home.

Your disobedient wife,
Eudora Mabel Carson

She took the letter and placed it in Esker's hand. "I want you to mail this for me. I know myself well enough to fear that my courage would falter and I would fail."

Esker nodded. "What have you written, Eudora?"

"Read it," she said, and climbed the steps to the cabin. She turned and said, "Do you still want to marry me?"

"Yes," said Esker. "Yes ma'am."

CHAPTER 55

The rain had stopped coming by the middle of April, 1863. Esker daily dragged well water to the garden, and by early summer, the well rope barely reached far enough to fill the bucket. Eudora's appetite, which had waned during the more plentiful winter, had waxed during the time of want. Her belly continued to grow, and though some of the women in Hamerton turned their noses up at her, many had visited and helped her with chores. No further letters were received from Albert Sydney, though Eudora had filed papers for a divorce.

Esker served his monthly tour on the prairies with the rangers, and Eudora moved into town during his absences. They maintained their living arrangements, with Esker occupying the smokehouse. Mercifully, the troubles with the Comanche had slowed to a trickle. Most of the raiders were occupied with midnight thefts of horses and cattle, and unless interfered with, left the occupants of the little cabins alone. Cattle theft had become as popular with the Indians as theft of horses. The buffalo had dwindled, and the Indians had gotten a taste for beef and had become stockmen. Esker, too, had begun rounding up mavericks and branding them with the help of Mosey and a few of the other rangers. He was careful lest he be accused of rustling, but wild, unbranded cattle had become widespread across the prairies and in the thickets.

It was late August when they heard of Lee's defeat at Gettysburg, as well as the fall of Vicksburg, effectively cutting Texas off from the rest of the Confederacy. The catastrophes had fallen within a few days of each other. Eudora sat in the breezeway of the dog run reading a rare letter from family in the east. The news they shared was not good.

"Does it please you that it goes poorly for the Cause, Esker?" she said.

"It only gives me hope that the war will end soon," he replied. He pulled up a stool and sat next to her. "Eudora, no Yankees have molested us here. Only Comanche and the likes of the ones such as Lt. Gibbons have given us grief. Aren't we too busy trying to stay alive and stay fed to care much either way?"

"I care. And I fear for my people in South Carolina. Since the war started there, I do fear that the Yankees will be vengeful," she said.

"When the war is over, we can go there, if you want. We can take our child and settle there, if it makes you happy," said Esker.

"Our child," she chuckled. "Well I suppose it will be ours to raise." She laughed. "I can just imagine my stiff-lipped grandmamma dandling a little Indian on her knee." She put the letter back in the envelope and laid it aside. "No, Esker. I am too sullied by life on the frontier to go back to those genteel folk. Maybe when I am old, and I don't care what they think so much."

One day a large envelope arrived. It was from Galveston. It contained no correspondence, but only a notarized decree of divorce, signed by Albert Sydney. Eudora read it and smiled at Esker.

"You still want to marry me?" she said.

"Yassum. Right away."

They were married at a little stone church near the Leon River. Eudora had found fancy clothing she had packed away at the time she moved to Texas. After ripping out seams and stitching in a panel of fabric to cover her belly, she felt presentable. Esker made a tie from some black ribbon, and brushed his clothes and did the best he could to make a reasonable appearance. Most of the ranger troop attended, and not a few of the women from town. Mrs. Johansson and members of her church were notably absent, a fact which both pleased and amused Eudora. A reception was held just beyond the church grounds, as it was commonly known that a raw form of alcohol would be smuggled in. The rangers slouched against the trees, sipping from tin cups and bottles.

"Now, Esker. I suppose you will move out of the smokehouse tonight?" asked Mosey. Several of the troop moved closer to eavesdrop.

"Well, yes. I suppose so, but Eudora is so swelled up, I don't suppose it matters much," he said. This made the listeners slap each others' backs and howl with laughter. They had drunk enough that they could laugh at most anything and there had been so little to laugh at for so long, it took little to provoke them. Esker was glad to provide the occasion.

It was almost nightfall when the guests rode or staggered home. Eudora and Esker sat on the porch and watched the land to the east turn red and then blue with the failing light. Esker reached for her hand.

"I love you, Eudora Mabel Doyle," he said.

"Well, I am right fond of you as well," she replied, patting his hand. Esker flinched a little and let go of hers. She turned to him.

"Esker, you are a fine man, and I think you will be a good father to this child," she said. "But I have long since given up on the girlish notion of things like love," she said.

"With time, Eudora, I think you will come to love me." He looked at her with such moony eyes, she laughed and kissed him.

"Come to bed, Esker. It is time we got this marriage started."

CHAPTER 56

Eudora's labor started in the middle of an October night, in the midst of the first thunderstorm they had seen since the previous spring. Esker left to fetch the midwife, an old woman with few teeth, who always had a corncob pipe clenched between two or three of them whether the pipe was lit or cold. She groused the whole way in the rain, swearing it was the last birth she would attend, and that she was too old.

It took the rest of the night and some of the next day to bring the child into the world. When he finally arrived, Eudora was exhausted, though far from death. She had cursed Esker, the midwife, the Comanche and General Grant until Esker feared she might be damned as a blasphemer. The baby was a boy, and when the midwife placed him on Eudora's chest, Esker saw that moony-eyed expression of love on her face, which he had so long tried to elicit.

"I guess you ain't lost all of your girlish love, have you now?" he smiled.

"No, Esker. I love this little thing, and I love you too."

"I want to name him Andrew Jackson Doyle, if you'd allow it. He was my good friend, and he was a good man."

"I will allow it. I will call him Andy," she said.

"Then call him Andy," replied Esker.

ACKNOWLEDGEMENTS

I want to thank Diana Stokely for guidance and assembling this book and for her artistry in designing the cover. Without her, this book would not have come to pass. I also thank Tiff Holland, writer and teacher, who gave me a one-on-one workshop on the mechanics of fiction.

As always, the patience and encouragement of my wife, Anita Russelmann, were essential to finishing the project. I want to thank all who read early drafts and provided helpful comments, especially Lenore Kathan, a faithful and honest reader.

Finally, I thank the Texas State Historical Association, whose *Handbook of Texas* was most helpful in research. Further, two books in particular, *Indian Depredations in Texas*, by W.J. Wilbarger (1889), and the recent *The Settlers War: The Struggle for the Texas Frontier in the 1860's* by Gregory F. Michno, provided insights into the character of the war with the Comanche nation, as well as the organization of frontier defense.